T0095809

# NO BIRDS SING HERE

DANIEL V. MEIER JR.

BQB
North Carolina

*No Birds Sing Here*
© 2021 Daniel V. Meier, Jr. All rights reserved.

No part of this book may be reproduced in any form or by any means, electronic, mechanical, digital, photocopying, or recording, except for the inclusion in a review, without permission in writing from the publisher.

This is a work of fiction. All of the characters, names, incidents, organizations, and dialogue in this novel are either the products of the author's imagination or are used fictitiously.

Published in the United States by BQB Publishing
(an imprint of Boutique of Quality Books Publishing, Inc.)
www.bqbpublishing.com

Printed in the United States of America

978-1-945448-95-9 (p)
978-1-945448-96-6 (e)

Library of Congress Control Number: 2021930148

Book design by Robin Krauss, www.bookformatters.com
Cover design by Rebecca Lown, www.rebeccalowndesign.com

First editor: Caleb Guard
Second editor: Andrea Vande Vorde

# PRAISE FOR DANIEL V. MEIER, JR. AND NO BIRDS SING HERE

*People don't want poetry or literature. They want celebrities, half-crazy celebrities.*

Mix a dram of Hunter Thompson, a dash of Kerouac, a pinch of Tom Wolfe, a sprinkle of Palahniuk, a dab of Salinger, and a heaping spoonful of Scott Fitzgerald. Shake liberally, and what emerges is an urban literary concoction that rises to the level of the best road trip stories ever told. At turns ribald and violent, at others tender and thoughtful, this tale starts mildly enough when Beckman, a disenchanted dishwasher with literary aspirations, flees his dead-end job and his writer's block to hit the road with Malany, a remarkable poet he encounters at a used book store. He concocts his theatrical plan after they jump out of his dive apartment window and head through the Southeast in her rickety Oldsmobile.

Malany is not impressed with Beckman's dishonest PR games. But in the interest of selling her stash of vanity-published poetry volumes, she goes along for the ride anyway, funding the trip with her mysterious, cash-filled envelopes. As the mismatched pair travel deeper into Southern literary territory, they cross paths with an assorted cast of clichéd and yet not so clichéd characters, from a tattooed redneck biker to a wealthy sexual predator with pretentious literary fantasies.

Meier's storytelling hits the ground running with every aspect of literary skill inherent from the first page onward: memorable prose, vivid characterizations, and scenes that move incessantly forward with much rumination about the meaning of life and letters, whether from the viewpoint of gritty pool halls and rancid jail cells or between perfumed sheets in the rarified world of academia. Readers in the mood for a loveless, sexy road trip tale should enjoy this one.

— Kate Robinson, *US Review of Books*

*No Birds Sing Here* by Daniel V. Meier Jr. is the story of a road trip taken by Beckman and a lady he meets by the name of Malany. Both are running from a life they no longer want to lead, and both are frustrated artists. Malany has paid a vanity press to publish her poetry book while her traveling companion is intending to begin writing his first novel, as soon as he receives the inspiration and possibly the experience. Anything has to be better than working in a restaurant with a very strange co-worker and a clutter of yowling cats beneath his window. The journey begins with the premise that if you appear successful, others will believe you are. But plans go awry as the pair meets a cast of unsavory characters who have no affinity for culture, preferring to whore, drink and take drugs. While some passers-by are left behind, others take their place. Beckman is forced to flee on more than one occasion.

My overall impression of *No Birds Sing Here* by Daniel V. Meier Jr. is a cross between *Thelma and Louise* and Scott Fitzgerald's *The Great Gatsby*. No one is quite who they appear, all the characters wear masks, hide their history, and play make-believe with abandon. They also have several brushes with the law, and at times it leaves you wondering if the consequences of their antics will catch up with them. This book falls firmly in the literary category with characters that come to life but behave outside the boundaries followed by the majority of society. There are some real gems here and there, my favorite was '. . . the angry glances of Hispanic maids pushing baby strollers which held the inheritors of vast fortunes.' I liked the excellent descriptions of small-town America and the story unfolds at a satisfying pace. It's impossible not to keep reading to find out what will happen to them all in the end. A very different book from Meier's first novel and an unexpected scenario that lovers of books that dive beneath the perceived surface of society will enjoy.

— Lucinda E. Clark for *Reader's Favorite*

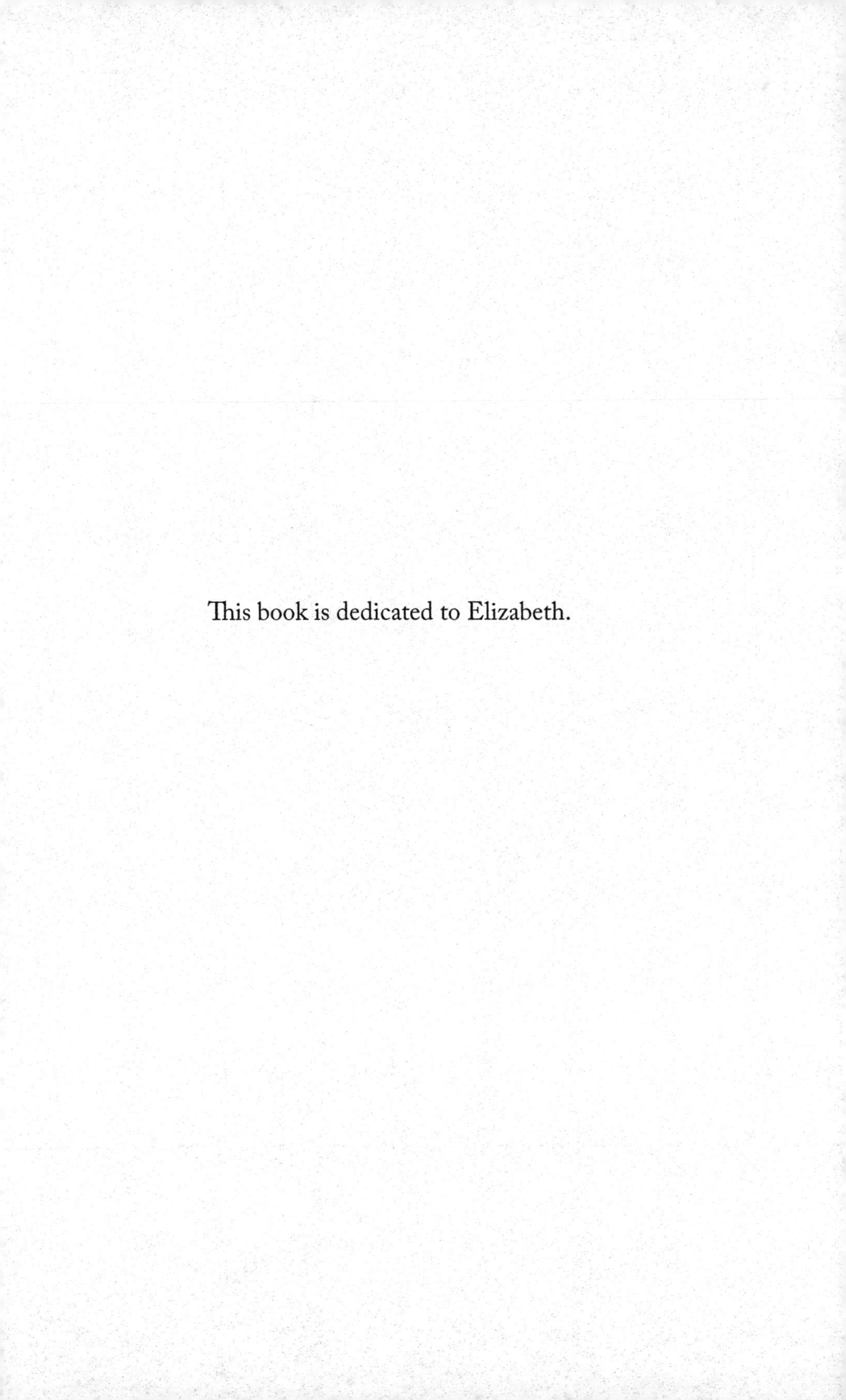

This book is dedicated to Elizabeth.

# ACKNOWLEDGMENTS

Caleb Guard, my editor, for his professionalism and assistance.

Jane Knuth, of the Knuth Agency, for reading the typescript, and for her encouragement and invaluable advice.

Teeja Meier for her faith, patience, endurance, suggestions, hard work, and love.

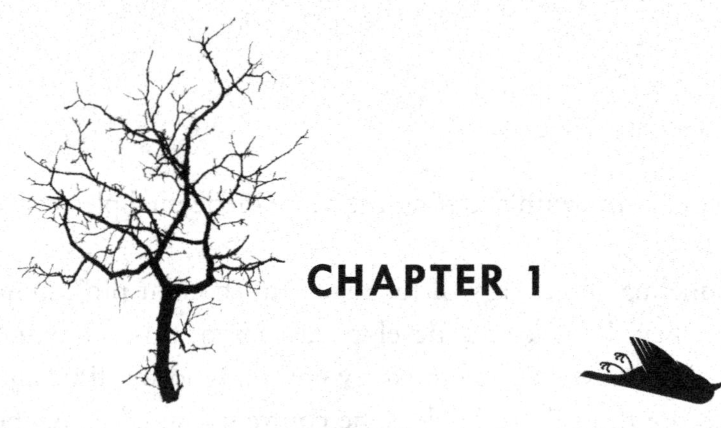

# CHAPTER 1

"*Quiet!*" Beckman projected through the cloudy, dirt-streaked window glass to the cats in the alley below. Almost every day now for the past month they had met at the same time, at the same spot, to square off and defend their strand of dented, slime-lined garbage cans. At first, he had watched the cats, fascinated with their determination, their pure jungle ferocity. They didn't waste time yowling in those days. It was a quick warning scream, almost inaudible, then the thumping of tightly muscled flesh on the ground, the rattling of old newspapers, and garbage can clanging against garbage can. Two grown men could not have made as much noise tearing one another's throats out. But now, after many battles, after they had shredded each other's ears and streaked their faces with Frankenstein scars, the cats had settled down to a wary truce, content to face each other on diplomatic haunches and scream defiance, yet realizing that further struggle was useless.

Beckman thought that this would be an excellent metaphor for his first novel, just the thing he had been looking for. Often during that month, the screaming cats got to him. The very first notes would send him raging to the window to fling it open and shout down, "Quiet!" The cats hardly glanced up. It was apparent that they were somewhere outside of his control. He could have used violence, but the thought sickened him. At times he had wished for some unseen demon to take charge of his body, only for a few minutes, so that he could send down a deterring ball of water. Nothing like that happened. No demons, or angels for that matter, came and he grew tired and bored with shouting the same ineffectual plea every morning.

By channeling the energy of his rage into thought projection, Beckman believed he could develop his mind this way, and possibly take the next step in human evolution. Ignoring time and trying to ignore the pain in his legs, he continued standing at the window, mentally projecting *Quiet!* until the cats gradually ambled away.

Beckman was pleased, even happy. He was sure that those thumping knots of cells and tissue in the center of their skulls had been made slightly feverish by his effort. The cats did seem a little disoriented as they left. He went back to his old, portable Remington typewriter that he had bought for $40 at a thrift store. He could not afford one of those new home computers put out by IBM, and he would need a printer, which he also could not afford. Nevertheless, he fully intended to start his first novel if he had to do it by hand. He had what he believed to be his best idea yet, but it had been interrupted yesterday by his co-worker, Herschel.

It had taken Beckman weeks to teach Herschel that dishes must be cleaned in more than one spot, or that the entire floor must be cleaned and not just where he stood. It wasn't until Beckman honestly thought that Herschel could be trusted to do his work alone, that he caught him urinating on the dishwashing sink. Beckman lost control and inadvertently contributed to Herschel's vocabulary.

Herschel even repeated the words for an hour afterward: "Stupid bassard, ton bitch, imacel."

The next morning, Beckman caught Herschel standing in the middle of the small kitchen, spraying a circle of urine around the room. Beckman backed away, staying out of sight. There was something ceremonial about the way he was doing it; a solitary ritual, as though some primitive declaration moved without restraint in his mind. Beckman peeked through the cracked door. Herschel was doing a strange dance on his toes, arms raised above his head.

When the ritual was complete, he walked to his stool in the corner where he waited between chores. Beckman thought it was time. He entered the kitchen sonorously and with some exaggeration, appeared shocked at the ring of urine on the floor, which was now starting to run in converging streams toward the floor drain. He pretended anger, but Herschel, with omnificent impenetrability, looked as insular as a priest who had just performed Mass. Beckman decided to use cold water to keep down the smell. He attached the rubber hose to a wall faucet, then pointed out every act of the cleansing process to Herschel. He warned him, in what he knew to be wasted effort, not to do it again.

"It's a no-no," he said, adding a mock demonstration of urinating. "A no-no!"

Herschel shook his head vigorously and gazed at Beckman, dull-eyed, flashing inscrutable grins that exposed his rotting and missing teeth.

Later, after closing, when the boss and customers had gone, Beckman, finishing his work, looked up into the soft, waxy face of Herschel, then down at the twisted, underdeveloped penis Herschel held lovingly in his hand. He continued to stare incredulously at the stream of hot liquid spurting forth with all the force of religious zeal, dashing against his leg, bathing and baptizing.

Beckman leapt back in horror. The liquid soaking through his pants seemed to scald the raw and repelled flesh of his leg. He ran from Herschel and up the stairs to his room, slammed the door, locked it, and continued running, tears streaming down his cheeks, to the closet-like bathroom near his writing desk. He peeled off his pants, thrust them into the shower, turned the water on full blast, and leapt in after them. He thought of throwing the pants away, but that would leave him with only two pair, one of which he saved for those few times when he could afford a movie. He stomped on the pants like a sumo wrestler until he had pounded them flat against the contours of the shower floor. He picked them up with his fingers, letting the shower spray bludgeon them into melting shapes. He wrung them until the fabric paled, ground them between his hands, dropped them back down on the shower floor, stomped them again, yelled, cursed, and wished with all his heart that Herschel would find a high voltage electric socket to urinate in.

Beckman turned the shower off when the water started to get cold. He had stomped and brutalized his pants until they lay at his feet as grotesque as a mutilated accident victim. He realized then that he had forgotten to take the rest of his clothes off, and his shirt, clinging and dripping, was beginning to cool with the rapidity of a switched-on deep freezer.

He pulled off his sodden woolen socks along with the rest of his clothes and lay them all next to the pants. He patted his body with a damp, sour towel and walked, half dazed, to his cot. He sat on the edge, shivering for a long time, steeped in wordless disgust at his present condition in life, and especially with his own body. He looked at his own penis and wondered how such a thing could have become the symbolic representation of half the world's obsessions; and now Herschel, stumbling around in the murky world of the mentally defective, had discovered his own symbolic, as well as ritual use for it.

Beckman wrapped himself in the covers of his cot. Waves of uncontrollable shuddering passed through his body like electrical currents. He had really never thought about leaving Baltimore, or of leaving the restaurant since he got the job a month before. In fact, he had come to regard it as a kind of sanctuary. He did his work uncomplainingly, even, at times, happily scraping the residue left in plates, on floors, commodes, everything left or abandoned at the end of its usefulness. He did this work joyfully, feeling that it was the most necessary practical work to be done, underrated and undervalued.

At moments, when feelings of revulsion swept over him, he deliberately, with eyes open, reached into the nearest full garbage can and squeezed between his fingers the raw materials of his livelihood. But now there was Herschel, completely mystifying, possessing some other worldly power beyond his touch, and approaching, irresistibly, the sacristy of his room.

He remained at the typewriter until past noon without typing a single word. The idea of the cats fighting over worthless territory seemed tired and stale. He put the idea aside. There would be time later. He was hungry after breakfasting on the last of his bread, and coffee made from yesterday's grounds. It was Monday, his only day off in the week. A trip to the grocery store was necessary, and he would stop by the used bookstore to see what he could find on psychokinesis.

The bookstore was wedged inconspicuously between a small grocery store and an expensive-looking dress shop advertising a special sale on zebra-striped nightwear. Beckman had a nodding acquaintance with the proprietor of the bookstore, an acrid smelling septuagenarian dressed like a caricature of James Joyce. The proprietor watched him suspiciously, following him with his old, hysterical eyes. Beckman, as usual, felt like a street thug and was tempted, this time, to stuff one of the ragged and stained used paperbacks under his own shirt but decided against it. The old man did have periods, in the year that Beckman had known him, where he seemed to have a past with remembered hopes and regrets; and for this, Beckman felt sorry for him and would not add to his cumulative torments.

There was a new addition to the used bookstore, and Beckman stared at her before he realized that she was truly a woman, covered as if she were in nun's black. But she wasn't a nun. Nuns wore street clothes now, and if they did wear their medieval habits, they would wear sneakers with them. The woman was reading from a thin black volume, selected, presumably, from the two-foot high stack of identical copies in front of her. Above her, a sign tacked to the bookshelves announced an autograph sale of poems by "Malany". Beckman picked up one of the volumes.

"Free verse, experimental stuff, of course," Beckman said.

The poetess seemed puzzled.

"Will you be here later tomorrow? I don't have the money now."

"How late?" she asked.

"After seven."

"No," she said, taking the volume out of his hands.

Beckman wasn't the slightest bit offended—the depersonalizing aspect of recent poverty and dissociation.

"I'm a writer also."

"Oh?" Her nose wrinkled from the sudden whiff of onions and old grease drifting across the three feet of space between them.

"Bullshit," she said.

"I love it."

"What, bullshit?"

"Uninhibitedness. Writers should be uninhibited. We are the only free people left. The last endangered species not on the endangered list, but that's where they want us, isn't it?"

"More bullshit," she said.

"Yeah, but . . ." Beckman sensed something terrible and turned to face the proprietor. He momentarily retched from the old man's hot dog-breath.

"I'm looking for a book on psychokinesis."

The old man backed away, repeating in what sounded like Gregorian chant, "Psychokinesis, Psychokinesis."

"When you find it, save it for me." And Beckman left.

He was more than disappointed when the cats didn't show up the next morning, but he had to expand. At some point he had to branch out, tackle new and more difficult problems. Herschel would be his next project, the practical application of psychokinesis: no more experimentation, no more abstraction.

Beckman waited until he thought it was time, then slightly opened the kitchen door, forming a door-length slit with Herschel in the center. There Herschel was, forming a circle of urine on the kitchen floor, obedient as a hypnosis victim to whatever biological urges that raced freely in his mind.

Beckman thought of projecting a whole sentence, a command like he had done with the cats, but a single, emphatic, easy to understand word might have more effect. So, he projected the word *Stop!* over and over again until his pulse throbbed and beads of sweat oozed from his forehead. The boss came in, slamming the front door, and the noise startled him. The boss didn't own the place. He simply managed it for an absentee owner. He was a man well over six feet tall who walked with a slight stoop like a wrestler ready to lunge at his opponent. He had thick legs, a distended midsection, a thick neck, and a roll of fat around the base of his skull. Beckman knew that any further projections would be fruitless. He eased the door closed and waited for the next opportunity.

It came, as before, with Herschel, walking up to him while smiling sweetly, twisted penis in hand. Beckman had all the force and energy of his panic to help him now. It took every drop of discipline he could muster to keep from crying out, to remain steadfast. He looked straight into Herschel's depthless eyes and, with undiluted adrenaline filling his body and with the harnessed power of a fusion bomb, projected, *Stop, stop, stop* straight at Herschel's forehead. *Stop, stop, stop, stop, stop* until he felt the warm organic solution lovingly dash against his leg.

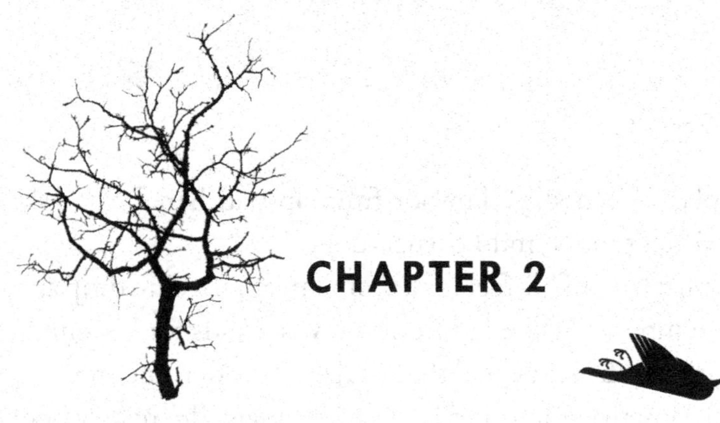

# CHAPTER 2

"Psychokinesis," the used bookstore proprietor blurted out upon Beckman's entry. "I spent most of the day looking. I knew I'd seen it somewhere."

The old man shook his gray, fleshy jowls. The skin seemed to be running off him in great, highly viscous drops.

"Is it important, young man?"

"Very important."

The old man smiled, and Beckman had to momentarily turn away to keep from looking into the primeval cave of his mouth.

"I thought it might be. Is there a number I can call if I find it?"

Beckman gave him the public library's number. The old man snorted with joy.

"Don't worry, son. I'll find it if it's the last thing I do."

Beckman thanked him and moved to the back corner where Malany sat among her books, talking quietly with a tall, broad-shouldered man. Beckman leafed through a shelf of mysteries and watched the man with a cyclopoid eye. The two seemed previously acquainted. The man was considerably older than her and enveloped in an aura of wealth and power. Beckman could not understand the conversation, but he concentrated, leaving his mind open for stray thoughts. The man handed her a white envelope, bulging at the sides, then reached down and picked up one of the books. Beckman focused both eyes on the mystery titles in front of him. The man passed, trailing an atmosphere of sweet cigars.

"Big sale?" Beckman asked.

Malany grimaced, then in jolted transfiguration asked, "Have you got a place I can stay? I'm not from around here." She asked Beckman with a tone of mild desperation.

Beckman, taken off his feet for a moment, felt his chin drop as his mind went temporarily blank. It took a few seconds for his mind to recycle. He rationally suspected that Malany's sudden and impulsive request had something to do with the older man. The poetry books filled up only one whiskey box, and he was unexpectedly pleased to discover that Malany owned a car which, thankfully, she had parked close to the bookstore.

The car, a 1970 Oldsmobile, was pockmarked from inestimable collisions, each victim having left a smear of its own body paint at the point of impact, but that wasn't what worried Beckman. Actually, Beckman wasn't sure what the source was of his mushrooming fear. Malany sensed the tension immediately.

"I just want to stay low for a few days, and don't think it's because I want that wasted carcass you use for a body," she said. "I haven't had physical sex in years, and I don't anticipate having any in the foreseeable future."

"I would not have thought that, judging from your poetry. Don't you ever get lonely?" Beckman asked, feeling a bit ridiculous by the question.

"My poetry is the only satisfactory cycle of emotion I need."

"What about the man I saw you talking to?"

"He's just a man, that's all. He's nothing, really, and he's in the ludicrous condition of not even knowing it."

"Is that why you asked me if you could stay with me?"

"Look, whoever you are. I . . ."

Beckman sensed that she, too, was projecting. He blanked his mind quickly, but not before he thought he saw a warning arc of electric energy pass through the darkness.

"All right. I won't pry," he interrupted. "You're welcome to stay, but you'll have to sleep on the floor."

"I prefer it, actually."

"But there are other things," Beckman said.

"What other things?"

"I get up early to write before I go to work. It isn't a pleasant job."

"No job is," she said. "Now, let's get out of here." She started throwing her stack of poetry books into the whiskey box. "I'm not going to sell any books here. Nobody comes in here. It's a crypt. Everything's old and crumbling and useless."

She motioned for Beckman to pick up the box of books and follow her out. He did, although wondering all the while why he did it. Did she have some mystical power of authority? Did everyone obey her will? He gently placed the box in the trunk of her car and noticed that everything in her trunk was somehow broken or torn including her spare tire, which was flat. She handed him the keys.

"You drive," she said.

"I haven't driven a car in years. I don't even have a license, and besides, the diner is within walking distance."

"Can you carry my books that far?" she asked.

"I don't think so," Beckman said.

"I'm not letting my books out of my sight," she said, taking the keys away from Beckman.

It only took five or six minutes to reach the diner. Malany parked her car in the alleyway, which frightened the cats away from their domain. She shut the engine down and looked at him with a mild expression of disgust. They got out of Malany's car and walked up the back stairway to Beckman's apartment.

Once inside, Beckman went over to a stack of wooden crates in a corner of the room and unpacked a loaf of crumbly bread, four potatoes, an onion, and a can of corned beef. "I'm relieved to hear that you don't rely on food to fuel your imagination."

"What is your job here?" she asked.

Beckman hesitated then said, "I clean up, pretty much everything. What I mean to say is, it's dirty and smelly." At that moment he decided not to tell her about Herschel. Chances were, she would never meet him, and if she did, Herschel would probably run, screaming.

"I may have to come in sometimes in a hurry and take a shower." Beckman continued.

She looked out of the dirty window, bored and disinterested. "What time?" She asked.

"Usually around seven. Will you go out at all?" Beckman asked.

"Probably not. I have some things I want to write, and I don't like to eat."

She appeared not to have heard a word. Beckman had only meant it as a harmless touch of conventional humor, something banal and standardized.

"But conventionality is meaningless and irrelevant," she said. She immediately left the window where she had been standing, gazing down at the ally, and went over to his books, which he had stacked against the wall next to the window.

"Paperbacks from the used bookstore, a few college textbooks, nothing very highbrow," he said.

But she was looking at the titles intently, weighing and sifting each for meaning, even the mysteries. Beckman left her for his two-burner hot plate to boil two potatoes and warm half the can of meat. He was beginning to realize, already, the shadowy complexities of two people sharing the same things. It was understandable that food and space had to be drawn in half, but there were other problems, considerations, or demons as he instantly labeled them.

"You strike me as a privileged little rich kid running away from Mama," Malany said.

"Almost correct," Beckman said. "Well-to-do rather than rich, and I'm running away from my father. He's a partner in a Washington law firm. He wants me to go to law school and join his firm."

"And you want to show him that you don't need him?" Malany said.

"I want to be a successful writer. I believe I have something to say."

Beckman offered her his sleeping bag. She accepted, immediately laying it beside his books. The act unexpectedly challenged Beckman's sense of territory. He felt in some primeval way dispossessed in one important corner of his room.

She consumed her portion of the food with bewildering indifference. After eating, they read for several hours, sharing the lamp. Beckman was hardly able to concentrate, before she stood up and began to undress. She ignored his stare, and Beckman thought the disrobing was a simple, deliberate declaration of freedom; getting down to the basic fact of nudity, the human body in its natural state with nothing left to the torments of curiosity. Nevertheless, he couldn't stop admiring her long, silken dark hair and the way it flowed around her neck and shoulders.

"Do you have a clean towel?" she asked.

Beckman pointed to the heavy cardboard box at the head of his cot where he kept all his clothes and linen. He watched her as she walked over and stooped beside the box. She was Eve stooping next to one of Eden's cool, lush streams. Beckman began to feel the tingling fingers of lust, that hated animal, which raised its spiny head, independent of his will. Malany found her towel and noticed his annoyance.

"You remember what I said about sex?"

Beckman nodded.

"It's a power I developed so that I could devote myself to poetry."

"I know, I know." Beckman said with a note of frustration in his voice.

"I won't object to masturbating you, if you want."

The suggestion completely evaporated his desire, not that he was against masturbation when intercourse was ruled out, but Malany had an unfair advantage.

"It sounds like perverted, orthodox Freudianism," Beckman said.

"Label it what you will, but it works."

"Pragmatism diluted?"

"How much have you written lately?" Malany asked.

"I confess not much, but it hasn't been because of my overactive sex life, which isn't active at all."

"Yes, but subconsciously, it takes its toll," Malany said.

"You may have a point, but suppose I don't want to cease to be a sexual being."

"Then you must be prepared to accept the fate of the common man, the common denominator of existence, enslavement by all of the servile, ego-generating forces which drive people into such symbolic acts of self-destruction as sex. Why do you think that the Renaissance poets referred to sex as dying?"

"Probably because no one had derived the word *orgasm*," Beckman said, thinking it might stimulate a humorous response.

"This dialogue is no longer valid," Malany declared.

She turned for the shower stall, her long, thin body bending like a delicate sprig. The sound of the water in the shower made him overwhelmingly drowsy. He couldn't resist stretching out on his uncovered mattress.

He slept until the next morning, well past the time he usually arose. Malany was coiled up in the sleeping bag in a fetal position, and seemed to be sucking one thumb, wrapped neatly in a thin membrane of white sheet.

Beckman dressed quickly and decided on coffee and doughnuts in the restaurant. Before leaving, however, his body seemed to jerk convulsively toward the window. Only one of the cats had returned and lay triumphantly atop Malany's car, surveying his Swiftian Empire with all the assurance of an oriental despot. Beckman did not have the energy to try psychokinesis, and he wondered briefly if it would be more beneficial to invert the situation and leave his mind open to receive whatever involuntary, non-directed message the cat might send out.

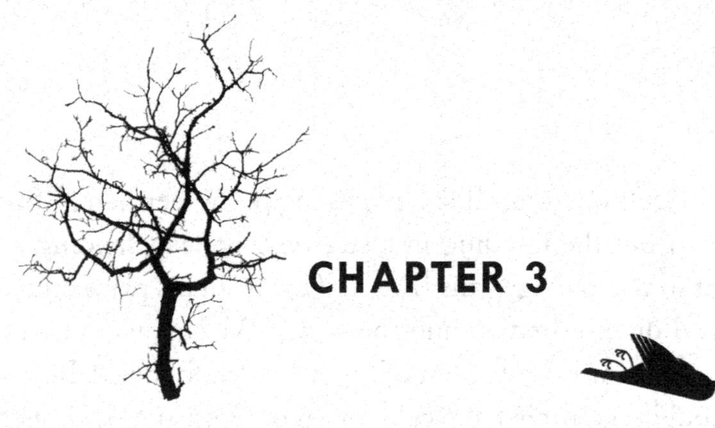

# CHAPTER 3

He spent the day avoiding Herschel, dashing out into the public area of the diner whenever he approached, being careful to lock the bathroom door, which proved to be a false security. Herschel, outraged, pulled at the door and banged against it, squealing with fury. Finally, something failed, and the door burst open with a crack. Pieces of wood were thrust outward, tumbling like small asteroids in space, expanding away and away and away.

Beckman stepped back and avoided the stream with amazing quickness, then leapt to one side and shoved Herschel. He fell back, forming a grotesque fountain. Beckman charged past and up to his room. He began throwing everything he had into his army surplus duffle bag, including the folded cot. Malany watched from her corner, expressionless.

"We have to leave!" he almost shouted.

Malany, without any visible sign that she was aware of the new tone in his voice, or that she even questioned this strange action, began to gather her few things. Beckman rushed into the bathroom for his toothbrush. There was a noise at the door and before he could warn her, she screamed. As Beckman suspected, Herschel stood framed in the doorway, twisted penis in hand, his left eye wandering to the left, his right eye staring wildly at Malany, who instantly slammed the door and flung open the window. With hawkish determination, and without a word to Beckman, Malany began throwing her few things out of the window. She climbed out onto the window ledge, glanced at Beckman for a moment, then eased herself down until she was hanging by her hands. She pushed away from the building in a suicide type leap, landing on her feet next to the garbage cans. The cat flew from his place on top of her car and disappeared around the corner. Malany was unhurt. Beckman waited until she was out of the way, then followed. Before Beckman could regain his balance after landing on the pavement, Malany had jumped into her car and had started the engine. Beckman, hesitating, couldn't process in his mind what was actually happening. Malany beckoned vigorously to him from inside the car and Beckman, still mentally paralyzed, jumped into the passenger seat.

It was some time later, after the gray-brown squares of farmland replaced the dirty, concrete blocks and red bricks of the city, that Beckman asked where they were going.

"Does it matter?" Malany inquired.

"No, I guess it doesn't. But I need money, and I hate like hell to admit it."

"I have money, as much as we need."

"Let's stop and make some decisions," Beckman suggested; and without a word, Malany pulled the car off onto the emergency lane, bouncing with terrific bangs over deep holes in the pavement.

"Malany, I just had an idea. I think I got it when my head hit the top of the car on that last bounce. Tell me the honest-to-God truth. Do you want to make it as a poet?"

There was such frankness in the question that Malany had to acknowledge that she was vain enough to want some sort of recognition.

"Short of a felonious act, yes," she conceded.

"It hit me just like that proverbial bolt of lightning. We're selling the wrong thing. People don't want poetry or literature. They want celebrities, half-crazy celebrities. They want to feel significant. So what do they do? Let others take the risks, and for those who make it, they bestow adoration and collective approval. For those who don't make it, ridicule and condemnation. The point is, what is defined as success straddles a line between illusion and non-illusion. People don't care, it's all the same to them. They want newsmakers, not people of unquestionable credentials."

"So, what are you advocating?"

"That we make ourselves overnight successes. Hit every hick town in the South East. You, a famous Californian poetess living in sin with a young novelist, me. I could do things like start bar room fights, and you could slip foul-mouthed quotes to the newspapers. They'll love it! I could play all of the popular stereotypical roles which say 'writer'. The lion hunting, heavy-drinking stud for the Elks Club or the cynical, wisecracking hipster for the college set or the lovesick romantic for the neglected and underappreciated housewife. Even the handwringing effete for the tea-drinkers of the Junior League. You could be bitchy and foul-mouthed, big-eyed and innocent, or weak and vulnerable—whatever image the situation called for." Beckman settled back with his feet resting on the dashboard, grinning for the first time in months.

"But isn't that fraudulent representation?"

"No, not at all. Although I admit it's open to interpretation." Beckman sat up, dropping his feet. "You've been to California, haven't you?"

"Once, when I was a child," Malany answered.

"And you are a poetess, aren't you?" Beckman didn't wait for a response. "And I am a struggling young novelist, even though I haven't finished my first novel yet."

"What about the stud part?" Malany was deadly serious.

"That, my dear, will be in the mind of the beholder. And, if asked, we will deny it vehemently." Beckman laughed.

"Beckman, I don't need these shenanigans. I can do quite well on my own."

"Come on, Malany. Those books of yours are vanity published. It must have cost a fortune. And you weren't doing so great in the bookstore."

Malany turned away, and Beckman was overcome with a sudden rush of remorse.

"Hey, I'm sorry," he said. Malany turned back around. "Look, let's just give it a big try."

Malany didn't move. There wasn't a blink or twitch in her elegant profile. Even her eyes seemed glazed over, painted in white vinyl. Her only indication of concern was to jerk the car's shift lever in drive and pull back out on the highway. Beckman slumped back in his seat. After some time, and after he had some control of his fear of Malany, he asked in his most gentle voice if she would take the next exit and stop at the first phone booth in sight, even though public phone booths seemed to be disappearing. No sooner had Beckman asked this than Malany swerved onto an exit ramp twenty miles per hour faster than the recommended speed.

The heavy Oldsmobile leaned and fishtailed on the ramp. Malany pumped the brakes, rocking the Oldsmobile back and forth with waterbed fluidity. Beckman watched, horrified, as the car skidded to a stop only an instant before crashing into a glass phone booth. Trembling, Beckman slipped out of the car and smiled apologetically at the service station customer, who had stopped cleaning his windshield to watch.

In the phone booth, Beckman felt that he had sealed himself eternally into a hermetic display case, and that the last thing he would see, before being placed on public view, would be Malany's wrathful countenance. This was only momentary, however, and Beckman started to punch the numbers. Some moments, as he knew, had all the qualities of eternity.

"Whom did you call?" Malany asked, ignoring the heavy truck and outraged driver who swerved into the next lane to avoid her.

"The newspaper in the next town."

"What for?"

"To inform them of our coming. I figured any small-town newspaper would like to have the story of the famous California poetess stopping overnight in their town with her young novelist friend. Oh, and I also made reservations at the Hilton Inn."

Malany looked disinterested and drove on.

It was after eight and not a sign of a reporter. Beckman picked up the phone in the motel room and dialed the newspaper office.

"Don't you think that would be a little obvious?" Malany asked.

Beckman held his finger up for silence and leafed through the phone directory.

"Yes, this is Algernon Becker. You might be interested in this. I just saw Mr. Beckman go into this bar . . ." Beckman ran his fingers down one of the directory's pages and stopped near the bottom. "The Dirty Sam . . . what do you mean, never heard of him? What are you, a fucking illiterate?" Beckman dropped the phone down. "That ought to make 'em mad enough." He started for the door. Then, sensing Malany's mood, he was momentarily thrilled that his thoughts seemed to come in with such clarity. "I'm going to this joint to meet the press. I'll call you if anything really good happens."

Malany felt decidedly uneasy about Beckman's proposals. She hated the idea of fraud and misrepresentation, but she couldn't resist enjoying the feeling of warmth that came over her when she thought about the possibility of selling more of her poetry. Maybe Beckman's point of view was right. Maybe, in the long term, that's how great things are done. How many national and world leaders have faked a crisis to get what they want? How many lies had been told in the heat of passion? She thought about the lies she had told her husband and the great lie she had told herself about not needing his money. She knew he could see through it all. He was a psychiatrist, a society doctor. He knew when people were lying and yet he wanted her anyway. He was willing to go along with her need to be a poet. He could be counted on—not like Beckman.

# CHAPTER 4

Malany awoke with a start. She had fallen asleep with her clothes on in the moon glow of the TV screen, something she never liked to do. The phone was ringing at a glass-breaking pitch. It was Beckman on the other end, sounding worried, and announcing that he had been arrested and was going to be put in jail if she didn't bail him out. He would furnish all the details when she arrived.

She heard him say "What?" to someone in the room. There was the hum of panic in his voice. Then the phone went dead. She hurriedly called a cab, grabbed the white envelope of money, and ran down to the lobby to wait.

Beckman was followed into the station waiting room by a policeman streaked with polished black leather belts bejeweled with gleaming bullets. The policeman glared with undisguised contempt, first at Beckman, then at Malany, who visibly shuddered. The policeman had some forms in his hand, which he threw down onto a table. He indicated with his finger that she should sit down and sign them before words could be spoken.

Malany scratched her signature on the duplicate, triplicate, and quadruplicate form. The policeman grabbed the papers, looked them over, and said toward the wall, "$50 and you can go."

Malany put $50 on the table, and the policeman snatched it up.

"Do I get a receipt?" Malany asked.

"Gottdamnit!" the policeman muttered and scribbled out a form receipt.

"Where is the car?"

"Whor he left it, I supoze," the policeman said, shuffling the papers and counting the money.

"I think you ought to at least take us to the car."

The policeman laughed, a wheezy, asthmatic laugh. "Get the hell outta here before I lock you both up. Buncha Gottdamn hippies."

Malany reached for the phone. The policeman charged toward her, hand on his pistol.

"I said, get outta here!"

Beckman grabbed her by the hand and pulled her ahead of the policeman out of the room.

"I was only going to call a cab." Malany's voice came from the darkness.

"There's a pay phone in the hall."

Malany grunted and Beckman realized he was squeezing her hand too hard.

The cab took them to where Beckman had left the car parked outside the bar.

"I didn't know it was a redneck joint, but what was I to do? It seemed all right until after about twenty minutes when I had started to give up all hope. This redneck walks up and starts trying to provoke me. You know, the bit about being a long-haired hippie freak and so on. Said I was too old to act like a candy-assed college boy. I tried to reason with him. I soon saw that it wasn't going to work, so I tried to excuse myself. That only excited him more. The next thing I knew, fists were swinging, chairs flying, and I was on the floor crawling like hell for the door. I didn't make it, as you know. The cops burst in before I could get out, and here I am. They hauled everyone to the drunk tank. The reds all swore that I had started it, that I had tried to sell them grass. It was terrible."

Malany was silent. Bursts of passing headlights flashed across her face. "Are you hurt?"

"No, not even my pride."

"I think you'd better cut the macho bit. In fact, this whole con scheme is beginning to look rather ludicrous. How far do you think you can go conning the public, anyway?"

"Malany, that sounds incredibly naive. The whole economic system in this country is based on the ability of one guy to out-con the other. Why do you think so much money is spent on PR and advertising? Look at all the great con men. Henry Ford, the Rockefellers, and there is no greater con man than a fiction writer. Yes, and even poets. I'll bet even T.S. Eliot laughed on the way to the bank he worked in."

"I still don't want to do it this way. It's inherently dishonest. Where will it lead?"

"Christ, leave it to a starving poet to talk about honesty. Tell you what, let's try one more approach, strictly highbrow this time."

Malany withheld her consent until they were halfway across the parking lot of the Hilton Inn. Then she stopped and looked with fear and shock into the darkness.

"But it can't be in this town," Beckman continued, unaware of any change in Malany. Halfway through dinner in the hotel restaurant, he noticed she trembled slightly, and her eyes sparked and darted with alarm.

After dinner she left abruptly, saying she wanted to go for a walk, that she would meet him back in the room. It had the tone of a command, but with an added dash of urgency. Beckman had plans to make, and welcomed the chance to be alone. Perhaps she was fighting a sudden, perverse desire for a rare steak.

He picked up a road map of the Southeastern United States in the lobby and took the elevator up to the top floor. He fell asleep studying the map and did not wake up until Malany returned. He wasn't completely awake even then. She said something to him, then undressed to take a shower. The sound of the splashing water lulled Beckman back into unconsciousness, and it was Malany who woke him, fully dressed and anxious.

"Let's go," she said, meaning now.

# CHAPTER 5

They headed south along Interstate 81, snaking gracefully through rising mountains, the air heavy with the odor of apple trees, pesticides, and diesel trucks. The sun grew hotter and more irritating with every sixty miles. Malany seemed to grow more uncomfortable the farther south they traveled, like a watchful animal outside of its territory. They cruised past unpainted shacks with black families sitting around, silent and idle, gaunt or fat white men in tight, synthetic clothes. Fertile ground for a literary society, Beckman insisted, as he reminded her in an unpunctuated monologue on the literary tradition of the South. They drove until late in the afternoon, scouting every small town along the way until Beckman, with unashamed joy, announced that they had found it: a town of about thirty thousand with historical monuments praising the dead soldiers of the Confederacy; clean, shady streets; and old established homes that Beckman was certain contained at least one grotesque result of an incestuous relationship. They drove around the town, mesmerized, until Beckman demanded to know the time.

"Four-thirty," Malany said, staring at her watch.

"Just in time to make it to the library."

An octogenarian woman in a flower-trimmed hat gave them directions in a screaming voice.

"Look at that," Malany said, her eyes following up the length of each Corinthian column. "It's a house, a mansion."

"No, Malany, you're forgetting. It's a museum, a shrine, an image."

"Oh," Malany said. She seemed to understand.

Beckman dug out one of Malany's books.

"What are you going to do?"

Beckman hopped out of the car. "I'm going to challenge the image."

"No fights," she shouted after him. Beckman jammed the thin volume under his shirt against his back where it would not be noticeable and strode in past the desk, commanded by a gaunt, gray-haired woman of inestimable age, then under an ancient, glass ceiling light, and past wide, red carpeted stairs ascending to the floor above. He went directly to the outdated card catalogue drawers and found the poetry section. He took one of the strips of white paper provided for notes and placed it neatly in his shirt pocket.

The poetry volumes were kept near the back of one of the largest rooms in the library. He took out one of the newer volumes and examined the call number. It had been hand printed in black ink, and the label was of the same quality paper as the slip of note paper in his shirt pocket.

He went to the other side of the room where it was darkest and carefully removed the clear tape which held the call number to the spine of the book, wadded the number into a tiny ball, and put it into his pants pocket. He returned to the card catalogue and tried the pens. The ink was similar, only a little lighter shade than that which was used for the call number. Beckman practiced printing the rounded letters and numbers of the library's book until he was satisfied with his reproductions. He then looked around and noticed the librarian at the desk glancing sideways at him. He looked away, fingered his chin, and carefully wrinkled his brow to create the image of profound thought. He waited a few moments for effect; then, as though he had unexpectedly solved his problem, hurried toward the direction of the stacks. He stopped outside the men's restroom, looked quickly around and, not seeing anyone, ducked in.

The restroom was empty and smelled abnormally of antiseptic and perfume. Beckman quickly bolted himself into the last stall and put the toilet seat and cover quietly down. Carefully, gently, he creased the piece of note paper with the book number that he had written on it to the size of the original book's number. With the edge of the poetry book and his thumb nail, he tore the paper along the creased line. It wasn't as clean a cut as he would have liked, but no one ever examined a book that closely, anyway. Gently, he removed the book's library number and taped it on the spine of Malany's book. Then he taped the number he had printed on the poetry volume over the dark area where its original number had been. He then tore out the title page with the printer's name, folded it, and stuffed it into his pants pocket.

He was breathing indecently hard. The minute hand on his watch had only moved a couple of ticks. He read the graffiti in the stall for a few minutes to calm down. "Fuck you" was scrawled in foot-high letters over the cubical door, inescapably facing the sitter. On either side, infantile etchings of erect and non-erect phalluses all with oversized testicles, ejaculated bullet shaped semen in parabolic trajectories toward the door. There were the usual advertisements for "blow jobs" with phone numbers, sketched drawings of figures in sexual intercourse, and yes or no questionnaires of sexual performances. It was all too reminiscent of Beckman's past life in the restaurant. He unlocked the door of the cubicle and walked unnoticed to the poetry section. He planted Malany's book in the space previously occupied by the original poetry volume and wedged the other book volume farther down the row, but still within the same number series. Beckman then sauntered up to the desk and looked directly at the librarian. He smiled as she glanced at him. Her mouth twitched nervously at the corners. She finished stamping a stack of books and turned toward him, quietly offering her services.

"What do I have to do to get a library card?" It was Beckman's most pleasant, most trusting voice.

The librarian reached under the desk, brought out a small form, and floated it toward him.

"Just fill this out. Make sure the address is correct, and return it as soon as you can. And oh, you can also mail it, if you want."

"Could I check a book out now?"

The librarian's mouth twitched again. She glanced at her watch.

"Well, I'll have to get Mrs. Dowell to fill out a temporary card."

The librarian seemed deeply troubled by the complexities or the consequences. Was Mrs. Dowell a fearful tyrant, a sexually repressed, psychic monster finding sanctuary in the physical, material world of books? Beckman eyed his adversary, feeling the sudden heat of her fear as he mentally pulled out his gun and ordered her against the wall.

"Oh, it isn't necessary to go to that much trouble. I'll stop by as soon as I'm permanently located," he said.

"Oh, are you moving into our area?"

"I'm not sure yet, but from what I've seen," he smiled his warmest, genuine smile. "It looks like the sort of place we've been looking for."

The librarian resumed stamping books. "Oh, and what sort of place is that?" she asked.

"Something quiet and established, preferably with a high literacy level. That's why I'm here, in the library, and it's only our first day in town. It's a habit hard to break. Every time I find myself in a different place for more than a day, I always check out what the town has to offer intellectually."

"Well," the librarian smiled, beaming two rows of skeletal-like teeth. "I know you'll love our little town."

"Oh, yes. So far it's been just perfect." Beckman waited. All the categorical questions had been answered. The librarian had filed him under subject with a brief biographical sketch. All that was needed was a title.

"Are you one of the new people coming with the fertilizer plant?" the librarian asked.

"Oh, no. I'm afraid not."

The way was opened. Beckman sensed it was time to withdraw and leave the title blank until his next visit.

"Thank you very much. I'll let you finish your work. I've held you up long enough." Beckman waved a feeble goodbye and started for the door. The librarian started to say something, but apparently thought it wasn't worth the risk of raising her voice.

Malany had remained unaltered by her long wait in the car. "Explain," she said. The tone demanded compliance. Beckman told her what had happened in the library.

"Yes, but what are you up to?"

"Making a very desperate attempt to sell your book and establish a literary reputation for both of us."

"Beckman, this is crazy, this hick town. How did I ever get into this?"

"Herschel, remember?"

"Oh, yeah. But that's over. So, if you want a ride to Baltimore or anywhere in between there and New York, it's okay." Malany started the car.

"Wait a minute," Beckman shouted. "At least give it a couple of days. I've got a plan. Do me that much of a favor. And besides, what the hell's back in New York?"

Malany shrugged. "People, activity, intellectual stimulation, and safety?"

"Bah. That's got to be the most middle-class bullshit I've ever heard. I'm disappointed in you, Malany." Beckman pretended to open the car door.

"I didn't mean that kind of safety, dummy. I mean I don't trust these hicks. They're . . . crude and violent."

"Malany, you've cross-circuited your identifications. These are good people here, admirably innocent, gentle as lambs. You saw the place. I'll bet there hasn't been a murder here since Cain did in Abel."

"I don't trust 'em!" she said.

"I think you're being very unsophisticated, which doesn't qualify you to call these people hicks."

"Well, is there a motel in this town? I'll bet there isn't even a motel."

"There has to be a motel. Every town in America has a motel."

"I'm not staying in one of those guest homes. What do they call 'em now, B&Bs. They're all so goddamn Victorian. It's like visiting an old, sick aunt with grandfather clocks ticking everywhere, driving people crazy."

"There has to be a motel," Beckman said with more assurance. "Shall I drive?"

Malany nodded. Beckman walked around to the driver's side. The Oldsmobile started reluctantly, battery going down, and the gas gauge banging against empty. Beckman reached over and patted her on the leg.

"Don't be upset. We'll be safe. There'll be time to write. And in a lovely place like this, time to dream."

He stopped at the first gas station he saw. A man, brown, wrinkled and dehydrated, strode out.

"How much can we afford?" Beckman asked.

"Tell him to fill it up."

The man's face protruded through the open car window into the car. He smiled, exposing a single twisted brown tooth. Beckman stared at his hat, a large, brown, baseball type with a gold patch spelling out *Cat Diesel Power* on the front.

"Fill it up, please, with regular," Beckman said, surprised at the tremor in his own voice and embarrassed by the man's hot, earth-smelling presence.

Beckman watched through the rearview mirror as the attendant loped easily back to the gas pump and violently twisted a few handles. Bells rang, and the attendant, hunched over, shoved the neck of the gas pump into the tank opening at the rear of the car and, in open-mouthed ecstasy, pumped the gasoline into the car with a torrential roar. Beckman felt a sudden strangulating nausea swim up to his throat.

The attendant began cleaning the windshield and stared down, watching first Malany, then Beckman through blurred swipes of the cloth. With the brutal smell of gasoline and the hideous attendant staring down at him with a quizzical look of determination, Beckman felt that he had somehow been surreptitiously violated. He stuck his head out of the car window and shouted to the attendant, who was now on Malany's side of the car.

"Is there a good motel around here?"

The attendant grinned, his throat working to suppress a giggle. He pushed his baseball cap back.

"Nope."

"I mean, is there some place my wife and I can spend the night?" The attendant, now smiling at Malany, pointed in the direction their car was pointed. "'Bout two miles. That-a-way."

"Why did you tell him I was your wife?"

"You have to in these small southern towns."

"Ha, ha. You see my point." Malany was triumphant.

"Well, I admit no place is perfect. It's a question of choice. The redneckery of a place like this or the savage indifference from

Washington to New York. Where we came from, people like us are either ignored, laughed at, or pissed on. I'll bet you in places like this they love writers, and I'll go further and say that they'll even give you credit for the effort."

"Ha, ha," Malany objected. "You're a disgusting romantic, Beckman, basing judgments on stereotypes. A writer must see individuals and how those individuals fit within the contexts of their environments."

Beckman was silent. He did not want to fight with her. He felt he couldn't win; not from a superiority of mind or will, but because he would see her at the terrible moments of psychic wounding with his gift of psychotelepathy. And to prevent that, he would surrender first. Also, Malany wasn't really ready to go back. She was willing to give them a chance as individuals, but something was out there that she was afraid of, some absorbing attraction left behind.

The motel was a loose association of individual cabins arranged in a semicircle behind the main office. Rates by the week, the day, or the hour were taped onto the desktop. A fat woman between thirty and sixty and enveloped in an atmosphere of dirty arm pits took the money, squinting past Beckman at Malany's car. Beckman paid for three days. The woman grunted. Beckman signed everything she put in front of him. While he was doing this, she lit a cigarette, scattering smoke and glowing ashes.

"I don't care what you do so long as you're quiet and don't break up the furniture."

She dropped the key on the desktop and Beckman, feeling denuded by her unblinking gaze, cat-clawed for the keys, thanked her politely and left. For the first time since he had met her, Malany looked close to tears.

"Say, it isn't so bad." Beckman feigned cheerfulness. "You know how these Ma and Pa places are. It's probably clean enough to eat off the floors."

Inside, Malany yanked back the bedsheets and held up, like a proud angler, a wiggling, coiled pubic hair. She immediately began an inspection conducted in terrible silence, repeatedly flushing the commode, running water in the shower and lavatory, wrathfully ripping away the bedsheets and pillowcases.

"But Malany, it's more sanitary with covering."

Malany sneered and held out a faded spot on one of the pillowcases. "Oh, God. I never thought I would feel this way again, but I must take a shower, even if the water's contaminated."

She wadded up the bed linen and stuffed it into a corner. Beckman thought he saw the beginning of tears as she hurriedly undressed and rushed to the bathroom.

Beckman switched on the TV, a disappointing black and white, and sat on the bed, back against wall, separating him from Malany's mad, tumultuous ridicule.

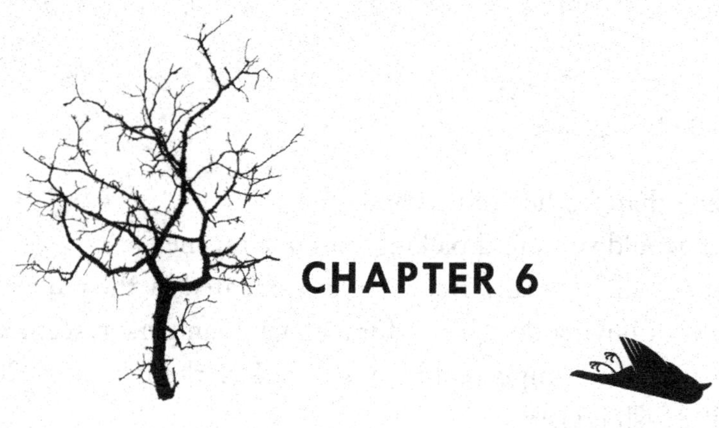

# CHAPTER 6

Beckman slept little during the night. It was not so much the canvas surface of the bare mattress or the mealy smell of the pillow or even, he convinced himself, the shadowy, silhouetted image of Malany's body beside his, but more that she had vowed, moments before falling asleep, to return to New York. Without her, the scheme failed; and without her, he faced the very real possibility of admitting that the only thing his life meant was washing dishes in greasy spoons and being lovingly pissed on by Herschel.

It was becoming morning outside. Beckman watched it happening from their only window. Then, seized with near panic, he slid out of bed, restraining his urgency so that he wouldn't wake Malany. He dressed quickly, floundering in the gray light and, violating Malany's purse for the car keys, he felt like a criminal.

Beckman dreaded starting the car's engine that early and, although it was irrational, decided to put it off for a while. He walked over to the office and was surprised to find it open. The fat-woman desk clerk stationed behind the counter seemed permanently rooted there. Her glaring, egg-shaped eyes still held the same dull hate, but something was different about her. She looked sweaty, and there was a cut on her right cheek. Beckman wanted to ask her if she had cut herself shaving, but he knew that she would not appreciate the humor.

Instead he asked, "Is there a restaurant close by open for breakfast?"

"Towards town, about a mile. A doughnut shop."

Beckman thanked her and started out.

"Mister, would you mind picking up some for me?"

"No, not at all." Actually, Beckman was irritated by the request. The thought of buying doughnuts for a gargantuan person seemed servile, wasteful, and simply repulsive. The desk clerk took out a $20 bill from the cash register.

"One dozen chocolate creamies."

Beckman walked back to the car. The morning had lost its innocence. He felt infected by the desk clerk's money. A stinking force outside of his awareness had once again touched him—undesired but unalterable.

When Beckman returned, the motel looked literally washed. It was the southern light, different from the poor light of Baltimore or New York; brighter, softer, less threatening hour by hour.

The desk clerk, overcome with anticipation, jerked her box of doughnuts out of Beckman's hands and began tearing away bits of cardboard and clear plastic, ignoring the change from her twenty that Beckman left on the counter. He hurried out, hoping to find Malany awake and leaving behind the receding moans and whimpers of the clerk as she stuffed one pastry after another into her mouth.

Malany was up and standing as coy as a billboard virgin in front of the window. Intense light passed through her filmy, white nightgown. She was a Nordic goddess. Her hair lay in glistening strands over her shoulders. She looked as pure as The Lady of the Lake. Beckman, in spite of himself, glanced at her hands, half expecting to see the hilt of Excalibur raised toward him.

"Breakfast." Beckman extended the bag of coffee and doughnuts.

"My God. I hate to admit it, but I am hungry. Oh, how I hate being a creature of the flesh; how I hate this body. It's always hurting and wanting, forcing me to eat, forcing me to shit, or that totally pointless reproductive mechanism self-destructing every month. I keep telling myself that I'm going to take up Zen seriously, and transcend this body, but I never get around to it."

Beckman extracted the food from its bag and placed it gently on the dresser along with ample napkins and several small packets of sugar.

"Beckman, I think you are the man-of-action type, after all."

"There's no need to be insulting, Malany."

"I wasn't being, really."

Beckman shrugged and bit into a chocolate doughnut. "How much money do you have left?" he asked.

"Enough for maybe three days if we live like troglodytes, which looks like what we're doing."

"That's enough," Beckman said, noticing that Malany enjoyed her doughnut. "I have a very good plan this time. Why don't you spend the day writing? That is, if you feel like it. If the plan works, you'll need more poems than what you have in the book."

Malany looked interested.

"Would you like me to drop you off by a park or something?"

Malany tossed her hair. "No," she smiled. "All I need is paper, a writing instrument, and to be left alone for a while."

Beckman started for the door.

"When will you be back?"

He spun around, pleased with her concern. She saw it and countered before he acted foolishly.

"I only want to know so that the anxiety of waiting for you to come bursting through the door will not affect my work."

"What will you do for lunch?" Beckman asked, imagining that he looked ridiculous.

"If I'm working well, I don't think about lunch."

"I need a picture."

"What for?" Malany asked.

"To put on circulars announcing your poetry reading at the library."

"I don't have one. Only the one on my driver's license. But I don't know where that is."

"Maybe we won't need it anyway. It'll be cheaper without it." Malany made a gesture of dismissal and began taking notebooks out of her suitcase. She had dissolved him out of existence. Beckman left quietly and, driving to the library, he reviewed his basic approach. He was briefly seized for a while by a contempt for Malany and by a sudden urge to keep driving. He thought of California and possibly even Bangkok.

Beckman considered it a good omen to see "his" librarian at the morning desk. She recognized him, acknowledging him with an oral twitch and a momentary glitter of eyes. She wasn't stamping books. She wasn't doing anything until Beckman moved toward her. She hastily began to arrange loose objects on the desk in some type of linear conformity.

"Good morning, Mister . . ."

"Beckman."

It was a juvenile game of pretense, and Beckman would play.

"Oh, yes. You were in yesterday about a library card."

"I was wondering if I could get a temporary one."

"Certainly," the librarian nodded. She was a protective mother, a servant of the public's higher need. She slid, with careful dignity, from her chair and headed more confidently toward the head librarian's office door. Beckman waited, scanning the notices on the hall bulletin board. A geriatric couple came in and, walking past him with sliding feet, nodded politely and turned hesitantly toward the reference room. The librarian returned and asked him to sign a rather elaborate card with his temporary address.

The librarian examined the completed card and asked, "Now, Mr. Beckman, what can I help you with?"

"I was looking for a volume of poetry. It doesn't seem to be in your card catalogue."

"Umm. Did you look in the nonfiction section under poetry?"

"Yes. Perhaps it's been misplaced," he said.

"Who is the author?" the librarian asked.

"Malany."

"Is that the first or last name?"

"That's her only name, at least the only name she will admit to."

Beckman followed the librarian to the card catalogue and waited as she methodically traced down the volume, muttering names and numbers to herself.

"You're right, Mr. Beckman. It doesn't seem to be here. I don't understand unless it's those colored children. You know, we've had to start letting them in and nothing's been right ever since. Now, mind you, I personally have no objections. Every child should be encouraged to use the library but oh, they are so destructive and so coarse, and their language, it's terrible. Well, come with me. We'll check the stacks."

"What did you say the title was?" the librarian whispered up from her position on all fours.

"*Song and Saber* by Malany."

"Yes, by Malany," the librarian repeated as she crawled diligently along the bottom row of the poetry section.

Beckman waited, watching the librarian's shapeless posterior, and wondering what secrets it knew—who had loved it and whom had it loved. It seemed suddenly funny to him that the planner in a pre-determined happening spends much of the time waiting for the right people to do the predicted thing. So, he waited, waited until she had risen to the crouched position of an Olympian sprinter to scan a third row of books. Then, as he had planned, she announced the discovery of the book in a voice croaking with restraint. Beckman and the librarian strode triumphantly side by side back to the center desk.

"You must really like poetry, Mr. Beckman. I've never heard of this book or this author before. She seems . . . very obscure."

"Oh, this is only her first publication. It received good reviews from the English faculty at Yale."

"Really? Do you know her? You sound like you do."

"Oh, yes. We've been friends for years. In fact, I'm traveling with her this season, until she leaves for Europe."

"You mean she's here? The author, with you, now?"

"Well, she isn't just outside."

"Oh. In town, then?"

"Yes. We're making a tour of the South and Midwest, trying to learn something about the people and their environment."

"For a book?"

"Well, yes, Malany's doing another book. With a rural theme and I, uh—it doesn't matter. I really shouldn't be talking like this."

"Are you a writer also, Mr. Beckman?"

Beckman tried to appear self-conscious. "You could say that. I have something coming out next year, but I'm not supposed to talk about it."

The librarian glanced to both sides, then leaned closer to Beckman and, in the manner of a fellow conspirator, whispered, "I understand."

"Thank you," Beckman said and started to leave.

"Oh, Mr. Beckman, here's Miss Malany's book."

"Thanks. Tell you what, I've read it several times. Why don't you read it and tell me what you think of it? Malany would appreciate your opinion, I'm sure."

"Why, I'd love to, if you think it's all right."

"Of course it is, and do me a favor. I prefer you don't mention anything about what we're doing here. You know what I mean; reporters, crowds, that sort of thing."

"Of course. Certainly."

The scratchy voices of the geriatric couple rose from the reference room.

"You see here," the woman's voice insisted. "Charles Mason Murphey bought the mill in 1870, and a look at the Confederate Army records will establish beyond the shadow of a doubt that he attained the rank of Major before the end of the war."

"That may be true, but that's as far as the family goes. His daddy was nothing but a horse thief and was once arrested for stealing a mare on First Street, right in front of the old Willoughby Bank."

"That's absurd."

"It's right there in the court records. I can prove it."

"Well, you will have to." The couple brushed past Beckman with surprising energy. The old man, pink-faced and angry, was in the lead.

"They come in here every week," the librarian said. "Local genealogists," she said with a hint of approval. "It's very big here, and you'd be surprised at some of the disappointments." The librarian allowed herself a small chuckle.

"Oh." Beckman snapped his fingers as if remembering something important. "I meant to tell you. Malany tries to attend poetry readings when she's visiting a prominent place. I didn't see anything on your bulletin board. Do you have poetry readings here?"

"Oh, of course." The librarian was indignant. "I don't know what became of the notices." She quickly leafed through bits of paper on the desk.

"Where do you hold them?" It was necessary to hurry, to create a feeling of lost opportunity.

The librarian stared straight at him. "Why, here. Downstairs in one of the rooms."

"Good. When?"

Her pale eyes alert. "Ahhhh, usually Friday nights at seven. Would your friend like to read?"

"Only if she's asked, of course, and provided it doesn't anger anyone."

"Oh, Mrs. Dowell would be more than pleased, I'm sure, for her to read some of her work. I'll see what she says, but I know there will be no problem."

The librarian smiled reassuringly. She had reasserted herself against the threat of equality. Beckman thanked her with servile politeness, just short of the comic, and started for the door, stopping there before going out, and looking back briefly to enjoy the sight of the librarian making her way to the head librarian's office with the seeded copy of *Song and Saber* in her hand.

Beckman found the print shop empty of customers. A young man dressed like a manager, and none too eager, kept looking up from his desk as though he expected Beckman to leave, which, after a self-conscious moment, Beckman considered doing. But it was a question of time now. Time had become important; not in the sense of an eternal concept as he used to think of it, but time as a limiting part of the present.

Since meeting Malany, he had developed a growing sense of urgency, and standing in the print shop waiting for whatever might happen, he became aware, just as though a genetic trigger had been pulled, of the finite qualities of all things. Was this the knowledge that drove people to print, or into a bank with a drawn gun or over a cliff? The knowledge of meaninglessness, the forbidden fruit of modern humanity?

The thought stunned Beckman for a while until he was startled by a well-dressed man tapping on the counter in front of him. There was a discussion about what Beckman wanted. The man didn't seem to understand, so Beckman printed on a four-by-six-inch sample exactly what he wanted: blurbs about Malany and the book, its price, a few additional lies about her background, and her appearance at the library. The man agreed to do fifty copies for $15.

"Can I wait for them?"

The man said that he could if Beckman wanted to wait three hours. Beckman said that he would be back for them at four thirty.

He stopped at a phone booth outside the print shop, asked for the society editor and explained, in an imitation southern accent, that "Malany, the New York and California poetess was in town, accompanied by her novelist companion and that she has agreed to give a reading of some of her best work at the meeting of the Poetry Society of the library." The editor asked if she might speak with this Malany.

"I'm not sure where she and her companion can be reached, but I've heard that they're staying with wealthy friends."

The editor thanked Beckman cheerfully and hung up. Beckman hung up and stood physically immobile in the phone booth. Something about the tone of the conversation had the discordant sounds of failure. Newspapers must be emphasizing truth and responsibility.

Beckman stepped out of the phone booth. Time seemed elongated; there were holes in it, and that made him nervous. He was also hungry, and now that he had nothing to do for the next few hours, he began to notice the hunger pangs. He knew that he had used his last twenty cents to make the phone call, knew that it would be a desperate gesture to search his pockets once again. Nevertheless, his hands groped in the cloth bound voids, fingers feeling seams, the linear forms of thread, grains of sand, minute balls of lint, but no money.

His pockets were empty, not even the most insignificant penny. He even searched the floor of the phone booth. Nothing. He would have to go back to Malany and explain everything, hoping that she would not refuse.

Driving back, he almost wished that she would refuse. He wanted her to throw a bitch fit. Any excuse now would be enough to put him back on the road, back to Herschel. He longed for something familiar: the morning ritual of Herschel, the cat fights in the back alley, the complaining regulars of the diner. He wanted to resume the daily development of his psychic powers and the trips into fantasy that writing gave him.

Yet, somehow, he felt that he had taken an irreversible course, a path to destruction that is the inevitable fate of those who are free to choose. Did he choose? Was he ever free? These questions stayed with Beckman, constantly repeating themselves, demanding answers.

He pulled up to the motel cabin and, with superhuman effort, switched the engine off. The world seemed in a gray mist of despair. He struggled out of the car and leaned against it, hardly able to move. The mental tape that his thoughts ran on had become a tangled jumble of spaghetti. But, after a while, he assembled enough coherency to walk to the cabin.

Malany was sitting up in bed, knees up, supporting a thick notebook.

"I don't suppose you've eaten?" he said.

"Of course not."

"Well, I'm starving. I have to eat something."

"As long as you're obsessed with it, naturally you're going to feel what you call hunger."

"Malany, I have to have some money."

"So you can satisfy your cravings?"

"Yes," Beckman spoke through clenched teeth, his whole body quivering almost out of control.

"Really, I don't know how you expect to become a writer as long as you put that first. All you've been doing since we left is grumbling, and I'm beginning to believe you like it."

"All right, all right." Beckman threw up his hands. "If you don't want to read your poetry before the local poetry society tomorrow night, okay. I've done what I could."

"You arranged a reading?" Malany asked. The notebook slid from her knees.

"Yes. At the library, seven thirty. You can probably sell some of your books, if you want to. Look, just enough for a hamburger. I'll get out of here, and I'll send you the money when I find a job."

Malany reached under the bed and extracted a $10 bill from the white envelope. She shoved it across the bed to Beckman.

"Beckman, don't get so upset. You're sounding positively manic, even suicidal. Take the money, feed your appetites. Obviously, that's what it's going to take to improve your physical condition."

Malany was right. After Beckman had eaten, his perspectives fell back into sync. He parked the car on the main street of town, what the librarian had called First Street. A faded green sign, strapped to a corner lamp post, authenticated it. Buildings, looking out from plastic and glass facades of the last decade, still had the architectural charm of the more substantial facades of the 1890s. Even some of the original names, those nearest the top of these buildings, remained uncovered. Beckman wanted to be sure to remember to mention it to Malany.

He noticed a bookstore after several blocks of trance-like meandering. It was a long room slightly wider than the entrance door, and appeared to be operated by a paraplegic. The merchandise was mostly paperbacks, new and used. The proprietor wheeled his chair through the narrow spaces.

"Only the cockroaches can move faster," he said, openly sarcastic and without humor.

"Do you even have room for cockroaches?" Beckman said.

The man frowned. Beckman felt a psychic surge. The man's hate was very strong.

"Something I can help you with or just looking?" The paraplegic manager said, sneering on the last two words.

"I was looking for something on psychokinesis."

"Psycho what?" the man blurted.

"Psychokinesis."

"What is that, some kind of occult stuff?"

"No," Beckman exaggerated a tone of patience and consideration. "To put it simply, it's the study of mind over matter."

"*Hah!* That's the last thing anyone needs around here. Everyone would be dead in an hour."

The man smiled and waited for effect. He was the local jester, safe in his wheelchair, denuded of a noble self-image, ignored and isolated, allowed the luxury of his cynicism. Even a paraplegic was not totally immune, however. He had his limits, like Voltaire. The wrong word to the wrong ego, and he would know what real power could do.

"Do you have anything?" Beckman stared, fascinated with the sheer physical grotesqueness of the man.

The man, smitten by Beckman's directness as well as his morbid fascination, twisted his face into a heap of wrinkles. His eyes bulged dangerously out.

"I don't know!" He all but screeched. "I'll have to look."

Beckman glanced at his watch. "I don't have time now, but I'll be back tomorrow."

The man slammed his tiny, withered fist down on the arm of his chair. "Why must I be tormented so?" he shouted after Beckman. But Beckman had already closed the door and was striding to the car.

Beckman began his advertising blitz by allowing Malany's car to be violated by the same mono-toothed gas station attendant.

When the man had finished and stood breathing heavily next to the window, with dirty outstretched palm, Beckman shoved the money into it along with several of the newly printed leaflets. He watched as the automobile rapist counted the money, then stared with bewildered amusement at the announcement of Malany's poetry reading.

It was too late to start seriously circulating them; and if she could, Malany would be eating a dinner of concentrated vitamins and energy supplements. The thought of eating instantly formed a glossy mental image of a fat cheeseburger spiced with a half inch slab of onion, an inch slice of red tomato, bright green lettuce sprinkled with droplets of water; tangy, eggy mayonnaise, and a frosty mug of beer. He drove around randomly until he found what he felt would be the right place. It was a block away from First Street. A small neon sign over the door sputtered the name *Sandbar*. Beckman found a parking space behind an undatable Buick bearing a bumper sticker: *Put God Back in Our Schools*.

The place was crowded, but it was a quiet crowd. Muted murmurings flowed past him with Doppler fleetness. Several men at the bar moved aside to make room for him. It was their only indication that they were aware of his existence.

Beckman was still hungry, so hungry that he decided at that moment the worst possible death had to be starvation. The bartender, a woman masked in Cleopatra eyes, glossy red lips, and the non-permeable skin of a cadaver, stood before him, silent.

Beckman asked if her establishment served cheeseburgers. The bartender nodded. He promptly placed his order for their deluxe, as pictured on the grill's exhaust fan.

"And a beer," he added awkwardly in an absurdly loud voice, above the general noise level of the bar, toward the retreating figure of the bartender.

Beckman trembled with joy at the arrival of his cheeseburger.

The bun was splattered with dots of fat, and bloody streaks of hot grease ran down into his plate. The beer was equally delightful, an opaque yellow, with icy fingerprints on the glass. Beckman's mouth foamed wet as a carnivore's. Such was his excitement that he felt an imponderable desire for that first orgasmic bite. One of the tomato slices dropped onto the bar. He didn't stop to pick it up but, at the first soft feel of the bun, the tangy cheese, the fleshy, earthy mix of meat and onions, unashamedly committed his hunger to unrestrained flight. The first swallow of beer was a good, but lower peak, and each bite and swallow peaked lower and lower, but never really faded. The man standing next to him abruptly spoke to him with deathlike urgency.

"I was married a whole year," he said.

Beckman hesitated, then nodded to show that he would listen. The man, chalky in the dim fluorescent light, seemed not to notice. He continued, "There wasn't a thing we didn't do. There was hardly a night or day that we didn't try something new. We both read every sex book printed. We attended the porno shops regularly, every Sunday. We even made a trip to New York to see the Cathedral of Erotic Art. And then one day she was gone; the books, the paintings, all gone. All I ever wanted was for her not to leave. I didn't really care about the sex and all of the surreal antics that went with it. I tried to tell her, but she hated meek men, she said."

Beckman wanted to leave. He made a motion to move from his place at the bar, but the man's stone face held him.

"If she were to come back tomorrow and shit on me every day, I would still beg her not to leave. She would hate me for it, but I would still beg her. How else do you tell somebody?"

"Tell somebody what?" Beckman heard himself asking, but the man had rotated toward the new noise. People nearest the door were greeting someone called Motoe. Motoe limped around the bar room on a twisted right foot, enjoying the slaps on his back from the customers. The sound of his singular name reverberated about the room, bounding from wall to wall, seeping into every crack and hole. He laughed and waved his withered right arm at each eruption of his name. As the eruptions subsided, a space was cleared around Motoe in the center of the bar room. A column of light appeared from ceiling to floor and seemed to trap Motoe's disfigured body in its glowing cylinder. Silence fell like the silence following an automobile crash. Music from a fifties-style jukebox began; slow, swaying music. Motoe moved disjointedly in time with the rhythm, his one good arm reaching out of the cylinder of light, his face serene with half-closed eyes and open mouth.

The crowd moved and giggled. Then the music got faster, moving in rhythmic steps to the single drumming pulse . . . ba-boom, ba-boom, ba-boom, faster . . . Motoe, keeping time, writhed and flailed his withered arm in and out of the cylinder of light. His face contorted in pleasure or pain, his hips pulsating wildly, and the crowd shouting the lyrics in unison.

The place throbbed with rhythm, expanding and contracting around its nucleus, Motoe. It hummed with inner life. The collective psychic force of the crowd was too much for Beckman. He had to get away or he felt that his mind would be shorted out, that it might even explode out of his head. He might even be absorbed into Motoe's cell and be lost forever. Escape! Escape!

He slid along the opened space in front of the bar, toward the door. Looking back for a moment, he could see only flashes of Motoe's gyrating body disappearing at the center of the pulsating crowd, and a sound like the tearing, renting power of a rocket engine screaming.

Beckman left the bar in a hurry, ignoring what sounded like someone calling to him in the street, "Hey, Mister, where ya going? Hey, buddy, come back."

The rest of the town was quiet. The *Sandbar* sign buzzed and flickered incongruously. It was the only noise in the street. Had he fallen asleep at the bar and only dreamed it? Had he suffered some sort of mental breakdown? He even considered the attractive possibility that some alien spaceship had landed behind the bar and was using it as a base of operations. Beckman arrived back at the motel. The events of the Sandbar still held his mind. As he pulled into the parking area, he saw the polished, black limousine with New York plates. It was hard to miss. It was the same brand new 1981 Lincoln Continental that he had seen at the last motel. It passed quickly under the light of the exit driveway and sped in a blur of red, amber, and white light out onto the highway.

# CHAPTER 7

Malany was sitting in bed, hunched intently over a book. "Where have you been?" She made a face with a wrinkled nose. "You smell like meat and cigarette smoke."

Beckman ignored her for a moment. He flopped down in the only chair. "I'm only human," he said apologetically.

Malany looked disgusted. "More human than I realized."

Beckman pretended to ignore her.

"Oh God, Beckman. You're such a defeatist. I've learned that about you."

Beckman smiled and brought out the leaflets announcing her poetry reading. He told her of his call to the newspaper and his plan for distributing the leaflets. Malany was truly, genuinely pleased, and even though she said nothing about the composition of the leaflets, her eyes glittered when she saw them.

"Would a defeatist even attempt what I've done, and would he succeed?"

Malany reached over and patted him on the cheek. "Poor Beckman. You know, you're in the wrong field. You would make a brilliant conman. Sales is certainly your forte, darling."

Beckman pushed her hand away. "There's no need to be cruel, Malany. You haven't even read my stuff."

"Oh, yes I have," she smiled.

"Well, you had no right." Beckman jumped up. "Where is it?"

Malany, in mock sincerity, pointed to his case. He rushed to it and quickly examined his papers.

"Don't you really want to know what I think?" she asked.

"You've already said. Be a salesman, be a con man, wasn't that it? Or haven't you had all of your fun yet?"

She started to speak, but Beckman, scarlet-faced, shouted, "No, goddammit, I don't care!"

Malany was unmoved, impervious to his anger. Beckman, feeling intensely ashamed, begged forgiveness with his eyes. She denied it, and then he begged for it with his heart and with his voice. He was on the edge of tears. Malany, cool as an oriental queen, offered her hand to kiss. Beckman, in religious humility, accepted it, kissed it, caressed it gently, and begged and begged like a monk praying over a holy relic.

# CHAPTER 8

Beckman scrambled out of bed when he realized that the sound he heard outside was Malany's car, and that he had slept well past the time he had conditioned himself to awaken since the age of twelve. Malany's car door slammed. Her footsteps on the gravel, strong and militant, came toward the cabin. She came in, breezy and unnaturally pink-cheeked, waving a paper bag with greasy spots on the bottom.

"Your junk food. Enjoy it in the worst of health."

"Why didn't you wake me?"

"You looked so guiltless, so pubescently sweet, that I actually didn't have the heart."

Beckman dug into the bag and started eating the doughnuts.

"Did you happen to pick up the local paper?"

Malany smiled like a lover. "Yes." She eased the small daily from its hiding place behind her back.

"It's on the third page, at the bottom, in their entertainment section." Despite this, Malany seemed pleased and anxious.

Beckman, his cheeks puffed out with chocolate doughnuts, asked if she wanted to help him distribute the leaflets. Malany quickly accepted.

"It won't be easy," Beckman warned. "There will be insults and disappointments."

"But you can handle that," Malany said with complete seriousness.

Beckman couldn't deny that he was elated with her confessed confidence in him even if he didn't totally share it. Perhaps it would not be as bad as he had made it sound. This was a new field, a field of creative action depending much on improvisation, spontaneity, and planning. It had all the elements of the adventure stories he had liked to read, but this included fraud, deception, and the horror of doubt. A true hero never had doubt, and if forced into fraud or deception against his enemies, it was always for a good and final result.

A gray, misty despair cast itself over Beckman. Seeing Malany at last happy for the first time since they had begun this journey did not help. He felt inexplicably hollow and, he had to admit, afraid.

She insisted on going with him and followed, haughty and triumphant as a Roman empress of the Antonine days. Beckman and Malany paraded through the one main street of town, stopping indiscriminately at every store and stand. Some owners laughed outright, some ordered them out with angry words and some, with skeptical curiosity, allowed Beckman to distribute the leaflets among the customers.

When they had reached the end of the street—that is, the part where the gaudy business of retail buying and selling tapered off to the hard reality of wholesale buying and selling, where weathered and rundown warehouses joined abandoned shells of buildings, housing only desperate rats and human derelicts—Beckman distributed what was left of his leaflets on the street corner. They were across from the bookstore of the paraplegic. Beckman was hustling the leaflets in newsboy style when a police car screeched to a stop beside them.

"Come and see, come and hear the poetess of world renown, Malany. At the public library, tonight at seven thirty. Come and see. Come and hear . . ."

Two policemen rolled out of their car and surrounded Beckman and Malany. The one facing Beckman stared down at him from under the black bill of his cap. One hand rested on his nightstick, the other on the handle of his gun.

"You got a permit to hand this stuff out? Lemme see what this is, anyway. Hand it over." The policeman stuck out his hand.

"Don't do it!" Malany shrieked. "He hasn't got the right."

"City ordinance 905 prohibits the distribution of any advertisement or solicitations of printed matter related to commercial or private use without a properly authorized permit."

Malany began screaming, "Rape! Rape! Rape!"

"Oh, shit," the other policeman said, casting a look of alarm at his partner. "Now cut that out," he shouted at Malany. She threw herself against the nearest policeman. "Rape, rape, rape!"

The bookstore owner had rolled out onto the sidewalk and shouted a litany of names he was going to call. Derelicts drifted out from their condemned homes to watch the confrontation. People from the retail shops began to gather at a respectable distance; cars slowed down with curious faces in their windows.

"Awe hell, Tommy, let's go. These two are crazy."

"We can send the wagon after 'em."

The two policemen hurried back to their car and left with much tire squealing and blue smoke. Malany was nervous. It had been an effective but desperate maneuver which could have easily gone the other way and turned the policemen into club-swinging combatants.

A crowd was starting to close in, some with extended hands, palms down, eager for a touch; other hands balled into fists. Beckman noticed the paraplegic gesturing wildly for them to come. He took Malany by the arm and led her across the street, pushing aside several red-faced, snorting men.

The paraplegic followed them in, turning to shout at the now dispersing crowd. "No blood today, you swine." Then he slammed the door, jarring the glass throughout the store. "There, in there." He pointed to an open doorway at the back of his store.

It was the room where he lived. The small bed was neatly made up, reproductions of Old Masters hung on the walls, prized volumes, vellum-bound, were dusted clean. A writing desk, antique table, chairs, and old photographs of the past were tastefully distributed about the room. The photographs immediately caught Beckman's eye. A young man, resembling the paraplegic, stood with young friends on a tennis court; everyone bore rackets and smiles. Pictures of him standing with friends at the beach in swimming trunks or standing with pride next to his new 1950 Studebaker.

"I've closed the store for the day. Things like that upset me terribly. The police in this town . . . My God, they're unbelievable." He wheeled himself over to a small refrigerator and took out an unopened bottle of white Moselle.

"Here." He held the bottle toward Beckman. "Would you open it?"

Beckman took the bottle.

"Corkscrew in the top drawer."

Beckman obeyed.

"I saw everything from the store window. The minute I saw the police I knew what could happen, and I was just about to call an influential friend of mine at City Hall when you pulled that brilliant stunt." He looked directly at Malany, his eyes rounded and moist. "It was truly wonderful seeing them devastated by a person of superior intelligence." He laughed, holding three fingers over his mouth. "I pity the poor drunk who gets it tonight."

"Poor drunk?"

"Oh, yes. It's no surprise to see a squad car pull up to one of the holes down the street and see some poor wretch dragged out and gone over. The word's probably already gone out about what happened this afternoon. The sober ones have moved out of range by now."

Beckman had managed, after considerable tugging, to open the wine bottle. The paraplegic leaned over to a series of wooden shelves next to the refrigerator and picked out three wine glasses. Beckman poured.

"Aren't you having any? It's really very excellent," the paraplegic said to Malany.

"She never indulges," Beckman answered.

"Never?"

Malany shook her head slowly.

The paraplegic looked at her pleadingly. "Please, just this once. I don't have many opportunities to celebrate a victory like yours today; and I must admit I shared in it—vicariously, of course—and I suppose, in a way, symbolically too. So, in view of our important event, would you please join us?"

Malany gazed at him for a long while. Beckman could feel her mental energy radiating through his skull. The paraplegic sensed it but, undaunted, he raced back to his refrigerator and withdrew a bottle of ginger ale. "Please?" he said, "please."

Malany consented, and together they touched glasses.

"Victory!" the bookstore owner said tearfully and, with a trembling hand, swilled the wine in offertory. The wine seemed to have an immediate effect on him. He breathed easier and talked in continuum of the "important" people in town, centering on their lusts, greed, lies, hypocrisies, and punitive criminality. He spoke as though he had repeated the words many times.

Beckman wondered if the paraplegic made a practice of pulling strangers off the street to serve as dumb subjects for his vituperations. Or was it done, as Beckman suspected, as a solitary effort while staring down at his distorted image in a wine glass.

Malany, shifting with impatience, finally interrupted to ask his name. He refused to give it, claiming that it was no longer significant, then added, "When my money is used up, my bank account number will become meaningless also."

Malany laughed at this. It was her kind of humor, and this pleased the paraplegic. Beckman sensed that everything about Malany pleased the paraplegic. He listened to Malany with an expression of religious ecstasy and, occasionally, it seemed, his eyes would move uncontrollably over her long form from neck to feet. The growing heat of his long dormant lust came to life as unexpectedly as a corpse, rising and pushing aside the dirt that covers it.

Malany looked with pleasure, on the paraplegic's disturbing condition. She even encouraged him with soft seductive tones, by touching his dead knee, by speaking certain words; words with *O*'s, so that her lips seemed swollen and sensuous. Beckman watched with horror as the paraplegic visibly shuddered.

"Will you be at the reading tonight?" emphasizing "tonight" and looking straight into the paraplegic's sweat-glazed face.

"I would give anything to go but—" he sputtered.

She touched his other dead knee. The paraplegic shuddered and drew a quick breath.

"We'll be happy to take you," she said, ignoring Beckman's signs of protest.

The paraplegic would have seen them if he had not been so intensely fixed on Malany. Psychokinesis wouldn't work under these conditions. The paraplegic was out of reach, out of sight, sinking lower and lower into the abyss. He would be a lover who couldn't love, a dancer on wooden legs. He would give all when there was nothing to give. The stupid bastard. Why does he think he can make it again, and with Malany of all people?

Malany wasn't unaware of Beckman's attempts to communicate, but she made no attempts to stop him. She had some inscrutable purpose for the paraplegic. Beckman left his mind open and receptive. He felt the sensitized points of his star antenna warming with reception, and although he couldn't get the image to take a mental shape, he had the sensation of something real and present, some dark formless thing called forth against the will. Was it one of Malany's monsters? Like all people who have monsters, she wasn't completely to blame. She had as much of a toehold on reality as anyone. She could make change in a money transaction, read a newspaper, and determine time from a clock. That would be enough to keep her going in the real world of rules and objects.

The other, that perpetual vortex of imagination and emotion, the hyper-reality, unlimited by time or object was where she had chosen to live. The paraplegic would have to deal with his own hyper-reality. This was where the monsters resided, in the hyper-reality of the mind, and Beckman knew that Malany could handle them. But what about this crippled effigy of humanity? What powers did he have to be resurrected? Was it a dormant part of Malany's self?

Beckman pondered this as he sat in the back of the room during Malany's poetry reading. The paraplegic sat in the front row, his head shaking slightly like a victim in the early stages of Parkinson's disease. He seemed to age visibly before Beckman's eyes, gradually sinking in his seat, wilting like a dry plant.

It was a small group; ten, possibly fifteen. Beckman didn't bother to count. None were young, and he knew this disappointed Malany. But she read from her book as though she were speaking to the multitudes. Only the paraplegic responded in the right way, shouting "Yes!" where audience participation was expected and remaining thoughtful and silent in moments of profundity. The others, unused to Malany's style, maintained the reverent silences of the sermonized.

Even with such titles as "Bitches' Lament" or "The Isle of Sappho," hardly a muscle twitched until the intermission, when all but a few rushed for the door, congregating outside to vent their rage. They crowded around the stack of Malany's books, almost forcing Beckman, who now fearfully scanned the semicircle of angry, distorted faces, against the wall. He really began to fear for his life.

The table tipped over and books scattered, with explosive force, into the crowd. One book, thrown out of the crowd, hit the wall a foot away from Beckman's head. Then another and another until it seemed like a barrage of artillery shells arching toward him. Beckman covered his head with his arms and dropped to the floor. The barrage slammed against the wall above him, and books fluttered down around him, sounding like flocks of wounded birds.

Beckman lay under the pile of Malany's books. Despite the continuing clamor, it seemed very quiet. The noise appeared to recede behind a transparent wall. Beckman pushed himself up from the rubble, brushed the hair out of his eyes, and was met by a man, red-faced, lined with an endless network of connecting wrinkles, and topped with a mass of white curls.

He shrieked, "There's no place for people like you and that other person in this town. We ought to take you both out and give you the beatings you deserve."

The face was replaced by another, screaming, "Pervert! Pervert! Godless atheists!"

A general cacophony of voices broke through the lunar vacuum and seemed to go on endlessly until, abruptly, it was again quiet. Beckman, after looking around, pushed the remaining books off him and sat on the floor against the wall, picturing himself as a surviving soldier sitting among the debris of his battleground.

Malany appeared in the doorway. "What happened? It's time to start."

"They've all gone. What you see here represents how they felt about your poetry."

Malany slammed the door. Beckman got to his feet and started stacking the books back into the whiskey box that he had brought them in. He had really expected and believed that his plan for success would work here, if anywhere. The explosive hostility of these gentle Southern people had shocked him.

Hatred like theirs was indelible and more destructive than the multiple fists that had been aimed at him in the fight at the Dirty Sam. He would find a way to recover. He still believed in the plan. He wanted to make Malany happy, but for the present, and that was most important, an event in their lives, along with its decisions, had been taken out of his hands. He felt in no way answerable. Perhaps it was the way a person felt standing before a firing squad; something deeper than simple resignation and, more purely, a sense that he was no longer responsible for anything, not even himself.

Beckman finished packing the books, making sure all the ones stamped with footprints were on the top. He folded the card table and returned it to the closet where he had found it, swept up all the papers and cigarette butts even though he wasn't expected to. When he went back into the poetry room, Malany was reading the second part of her selections to a room empty except for the paraplegic. She was reading as though the room was full of people. Beckman wondered for a moment if the shock had been too great, and if she had completely lost contact. He watched her for a while. There were tears in her eyes, and he knew that she was not insane.

He spoke. "It's pointless, Malany, even ridiculous. I'm surprised at you, making such a romantic gesture. These people are ready to run us out of town, and they probably will unless we get moving."

The paraplegic turned to him and shouted across the room of empty chairs, "Let her read, you fool. Let her read."

Malany, tears running down her cheeks, said, "Yes. Let me read. I came here to read. Let me read."

Beckman waited. The paraplegic glared at him, panting hatred.

Beckman—and he felt terrible about it afterwards—walked back and forth across the back of the room, showing his body and his precious legs to the trembling, foaming, white-hot paraplegic.

"I'll be waiting in the car when you've finished," Beckman said, stopping at the door and looking back to see Malany turned away, sobbing. He picked up the box of books and bore them in both arms with considerable effort out of the building to the car.

He had imagined that someone, unsatisfied with the thought that he had been left alive, might be waiting outside. But, to his relief, the parking lot was clear. Malany's was the only car visible and fortunately well illuminated under a streetlight. He loaded the books into the trunk and, knowing Malany would not be in condition to drive, got in on the driver's side, locked the doors and, because it was a warm night, rolled the windows down halfway.

He did not want to believe that there would be more violence, but he knew how deeply Malany had wounded them. Maybe the white-haired gentleman's mind would snap while he tried calming down with a drink of brandy in his library, and he might return as Mr. Hyde, bent on murder.

Beckman laughed. If he were back in Baltimore or Philadelphia, he would seriously consider that possibility. Then, too, he had been wrong about the local reaction to Malany's poetry, a consideration that he had given second place, tragically forgetting the only communication he'd had with his boss at the diner. "Son," said his imagined boss. "Words is power. Ask any lawyer." Beckman realized that he had mixed the wrong words with the wrong culture and ignited the explosion.

No, he couldn't blame them for being angry at someone who farted in their perfumed air. He had been naive and foolish and felt a little guilty for not remaining with that other cripple until Malany had had her great hour upon the stage. Shakespeare had thought of it all, so what was the use? At least a Shakespearean scholar at his old college believed so, and was so convinced of it that he had spent his last years in the artificial world of drug addicts, shouting obscenities from apartment windows.

There was a gentle tapping at the car window. Beckman roused himself from dreaming and opened the door.

“Can you hold him?” Malany asked, pointing to the paraplegic who was unconscious in his wheelchair.

“What happened?” Beckman asked, getting out of the car.

“I think he’s in a trance. He just slumped over when I finished.”

“Did you check to see if he was dead?”

“God, no. You don’t suppose . . .”

Beckman slowly raised the paraplegic’s head. “By God, he looks dead.”

“Oh, Jesus!”

Beckman felt the man’s pulse, then the chest area over the heart. “But he’s alive. Just fainted. Help me.”

Malany and Beckman lifted the limp body out of the wheelchair and slid him onto the back seat, folding his arms and legs into a fetal position so that he would fit. Beckman folded up the wheelchair after some trouble finding the right release points, and put it in the back so that it rested against the seat without touching the stricken man.

They rode in silence back to the motel and, without turning, Beckman could see her eyes in passing flashes of light. They were like the entrances of two wide, dark tunnels. Sensing her anguish and checked by guilt, Beckman begged her forgiveness in a torrent of words, blubbering forth in what seemed like the secret tongues of a Pentecostal. The paraplegic, by then awake and laughing maniacally, erupted into a fit of coughing.

Malany was unmoved, silent as a marble goddess. She never believed anyone suffered with quite the same acuity as she did. When they stopped in front of the cabin, Beckman reached over to shut off the engine but was stopped by Malany's hand. He had opened his mind and so wasn't too surprised as he had been receiving unclear impressions during the ride from the library. When Malany said she would not be going in, Beckman got out of the car.

"Where will you go?" he asked as Malany slid over into the driver's seat. She glanced back at the now sleeping half man.

"With him," she said.

"We could try another place. Somewhere out west maybe?" Beckman asked.

She shook her head.

"Malany, I'm a cripple too. It isn't as obvious as his, but I know it's there. Everybody in the straight world treats me like one, like I can't stand erect, or like I'm going to rape their daughters. You know. You must be aware."

Malany didn't acknowledge. She only looked ahead at the distant lights.

"All right!" Beckman tried to sound angry but couldn't. He stepped out of the car and turned to look at her through the open window. "I haven't got a dime. Could you spare something? I'll probably never be able to pay it back."

Malany held a $20 bill out of the window. He took the bill and looked at it, surprised at the suddenness and the finality. He wanted to speak. Something must be said. She was driving away and in doing so, jerked something out of him, took away something vital. He felt internally flaccid. He was dying.

He screamed, "Wait!"

But she was really gone, and gone to live with a paraplegic whose useful time had ended the day he was crippled. What had she chosen? Yes, it was Malany who made the choices. It was her money, her power that had created his illusions and made them seem real. Now that she had withdrawn them, and without explanation (did she think explanations were not necessary or important to him?), he realized the falsity of purpose, the stupidity of a "meaningful life". He felt, finally, at the end of something. He looked at the motel cabins, outlined by a single naked light over the office; the last stopping place for the rejected, the defeated, the separation station for an army of human derelicts.

Beckman waited, stunned for a moment by the night silence, then started toward his cabin. There was a sound; threatening, primeval. Instinctively he froze, the gift of millions of years of fear. Bushes rustled near his cabin. He heard animal sounds of grunting and effort. Beckman moved forward on tiptoes, feeling like exposed prey. He was close to the bushes. He crouched. A strange excitement had replaced his fear. His senses were alert to the slightest change; his mind tuned to wide reception. In the dim yellow light, Beckman saw a head emerge from the bush under his windows. The segmented image of the person's body became more visible through the bush. The hair was long, to the waist. It was the motel desk clerk looking in his window.

Beckman's first impulse, his wonderful instinctive self, was to stop her; but he had the advantage, and he was curious. The woman's head moved to one side. She cupped her hands over her eyes and seemed to press her face against the windowpane. It was very quiet, not even the sound of traffic on the highway. She looked around quickly, then jumped down from whatever she was standing on. Beckman remained crouched and watched. There were sounds of rattling leaves and twigs snapping. Then a muted cry, sounds of physical struggle. Beckman ran over to the wriggling bush and found the desk clerk on her knees, tearing at the bush with wild hands. Her hair had become entangled. When she saw him, she yelped and started kicking at him.

"Stop! If you'll stop, I'll help you."

"No, you won't." She kicked again when he moved closer. She held the tangled hair and branch in both hands and was now lying on her side, both legs kicking like a fallen bicycle rider.

"Don't you touch me! I'll call the police! I will!" She tugged furiously at the entanglement for a few moments.

"What were you doing here?" he demanded. Beckman hunched down close to her, but out of range of her feet.

"That ain't none of your bisness."

"I saw you looking in my window."

"I was not. I ain't never done any such of a thing. You can't prove it."

"Suppose I went in, got my camera, and took a picture of you here in your strange predicament."

The desk clerk pulled frantically at her hair, making a humming sound. She stopped after a while, breathing hard. "That don't prove nothin'. I thought I seen somebody sneaking around out here, a thief or somethin' like that. So I came to check it out. That's all."

"But you did look in my window?"

"Well, what if I did? It could be somethin' totally different from what you're thinking. I might have saw the thief go into your cabin. Maybe I just wanted to make sure before calling the sheriff. I was just looking out for y'all, and here you go accusing me of somethin' terrible and disgusting."

"I only want to know why you were looking in my window."

The desk clerk started to cry. "I wasn't. That's only the way it looked to you."

"Let me help you."

"Don't touch me."

"You can't stay here. God knows what kinds of things will crawl over you in the night."

"Oh God!" She was close to sobs and still clutched, but weakly, the knot of branch and hair. "There's a pair of scissors in the office, in the desk drawer, on the left. Please hurry."

Beckman trotted toward the office, still seeing the image of the desk clerk rolling on the ground; dress gathered around her mid-section, massive rolls of flesh, unidentifiable sexual parts, and featureless face. The office was unlocked, a possibility Beckman had not considered until he reached for the door. He was at the desk in two long strides. A shaded lamp on the desk provided the only light. Beckman tore open the top left drawer. Nothing. And then the bottom one. No scissors. He tried the top right drawer. The scissors were there, lying beside an old-fashioned scrapbook which was bound with heavy, brown, cardboard covers and fastened with thick, black ribbon.

Beckman placed the scissors gently on the desk and slowly lifted the scrapbook from the drawer. The first few pages were devoted to pictures of not very intelligent-looking adolescents, all in the forced poses of their senior class pictures. The middle part was crammed with newspaper clippings of weddings, birth announcements, divorces, court records, a weekly gossip column, and tabloid reviews of soap operas, all carefully preserved under a plastic overlay.

Further on, there were pictures of movie and television stars cut from fan magazines, and the last few pages of the scrapbook were devoted to glossy, color, pornographic pictures of couples, heterosexual and lesbian, joined in an ecstatic union, carefully pasted and covered with clear plastic.

Beneath the scrapbook, in the same drawer, were stacks of pornographic magazines, most with glossy color covers. Beckman replaced the magazines and the scrapbook carefully, and eased the drawer closed. He was moving like a house thief now, quickly snatching the scissors off the desk and stealing out of the office.

"What took you so long?"

"Nothing. I had trouble finding the scissors." Beckman crawled under the bush beside the desk clerk. "It's going to be difficult without much light."

"Just don't try anything funny."

"I'll try to cut the branch. Maybe we can save your hair that way."

"Oh God, I hope so."

"Don't move. Not even if a snake bites you."

The woman shuddered. Beckman cut at the smallest part of the branch, just beyond the knot. He tried to cut with the scissors in the conventional way, but the branch was too large and much tougher than it looked. He tried sawing with one of the blades, but that was hopeless.

"I'm sorry. The branch simply will not give."

The woman started crying again. Beckman found all the hair that was caught, separated it from the free hair, then flattened the tangled hair between his two middle fingers, running his hand up to the knot. He placed the scissors against the front of his fingers and cut. The sound was like tearing flesh. He could feel the hair giving way, like the severing of a tight muscle. She cried as though she was experiencing real physical pain. When the last group of strands had parted, she scrambled out from under the bush and ran away. Beckman heard her running, great thudding steps fading in the night, but could not see the direction she took. He twisted and worked the offending branch until it broke off, leaving jagged green ends, slimy with organic juices.

The cabin had not been entered. A few of Malany's things were on the bed—a comb, a pair of old running shoes, panties, and dirty socks with holes. Beckman rolled the stuff into a ball and put it into his duffle bag. He gathered up his own things and put them on top of Malany's. He double-checked the room and the bathroom to make sure that he had not forgotten anything. He lowered the venetian blind at the window and settled back on the bed with his clothes on. He would sleep in his clothes and leave early in the morning.

The green branch with the woman's hair lay on the bedside table. He reached over for it, looked at it, and turned it over in his hand until it became the only part of his vision in focus. The hair was silky, light brown, and looked like delicate feathers caught in a trap. It was beautiful hair and well cared for. If he had not known for sure, Beckman would never have guessed that it belonged to the desk clerk. It was hopelessly entangled—a Gordian knot of hair and branches. He tossed it into the plastic trash can.

A feeling of Malany's absence washed over him, leaving a sudden vacuum in the center of his body that hurt. He rolled across his bed and dug back into his duffle bag until he found his book, *Parapsychology: Frontier Science of the Mind*. The page marker was where he had stopped two months ago, before Herschel, before Malany. The chapter wasn't clear. He couldn't remember some of the important parts. He turned back to the beginning. A review of what he had read before would be necessary.

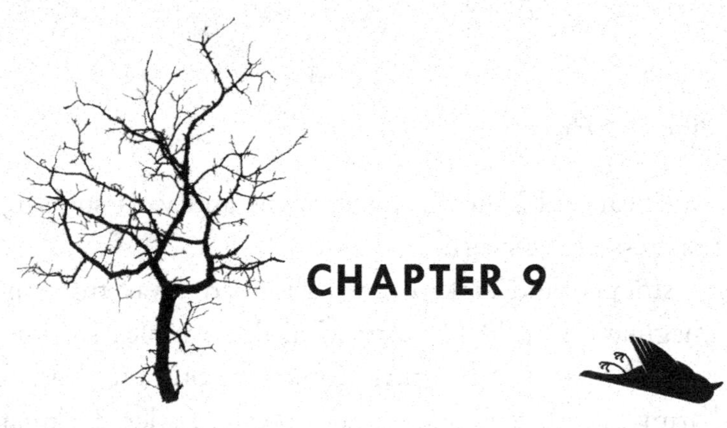

# CHAPTER 9

It was still dark outside when he awoke. His book rested flat on his chest, opened to where it had fallen. It was the same scented night that he had left in the library parking lot, the same night that he had freed the desk clerk. Yet it seemed like those events were far away, distant memories separated by an infinite chasm. The silence seemed profound when he stopped outside the closed office and dropped the room key into the door slot. He struggled for a moment with the question of paying for his few hours of rest. The question took the form of a hallucination, something grotesque but laughable. He wanted to wait and let the imaginative possibilities unfold, but he was overcome with a sense of urgency to leave, to flee.

He walked, for a time, along the roadside. Several cars passed, but he didn't bother to put out his thumb. He was happier walking. Each step made him feel a little cleaner, a little more ebullient. Hope flowed again and seemed to grow with each step forward. When he was ready, he turned to face what cars might be going his way and noticed, with almost painful joy, that it was becoming daylight and that there were no cars in sight.

A thin, sweet-smelling mist hung motionless in the air, veiling the trees and highway and lacing the grass on the edge of the road with droplets of water that turned into dark, wet footprints as Beckman walked. Beckman believed that, if it had not been for the paved highway, strictly divided and regulated by white and yellow lines, and for the trash deposited along the grassy shoulders, he could have been in some medieval forest, populated with knights, magicians and beautiful ladies in long gowns and veils suffering some quiet distress of the heart.

Beckman stopped and looked down the road, away from the light. His imagination could see, formed in the complex shadows and waves of mist, a parade of knights. Could it be St. Louis leading an ethereal army of followers on another noble crusade? Beckman had read about St. Louis and concluded that history's sainted king had been gifted with psychic ability and a defective understanding.

St. Louis never seemed to understand the power of selfishness. He was used and then abandoned by his brothers. The Knights Templar, considering him a bad investment, refused to loan him his own ransom money. Even his most faithful knights, knowing he was bankrupt, demanded increases in pay and an honorable means of escaping an unprofitable Holy War. Yes, Beckman thought, it would be like St. Louis to lead pure and holy crusades against the dark forces of evil and missing the mark for all eternity.

Beckman had walked for some time, thinking about St. Louis, before he heard the truck behind him. He turned and stuck out his thumb. Two headlights were approaching out of the evaporating mist. They were dimmed by the creeping sunlight. The truck rumbled past. It was an old-model, mud-splashed farm truck with two monstrous brown pigs in the back. Beckman saw the truck's brake lights flash on. Then the truck moved toward the shoulder, but not on it, and came to a stop. He ran toward it to show his appreciation but hoped that he could find a polite way to refuse. He opened the door, which immediately sagged on its hinges. The farmer at the wheel glanced casually at him.

"I almost didn't see you in this fog. It's awful dangerous hitchhiking in this mess. Get in before somebody comes along and rams us into kingdom come."

Beckman climbed in and closed the heavy metal door. The farmer shifted gears and the truck lurched forward. It was no longer a world of sweet smells, of mist and shadows. The truck, dented and scarred like the farmer, encapsulated the noisy world of machines, human bodies, and the faint but omnipresent odor of pigs.

"You ain't the kind that hits people over the head, are you?"

The question startled Beckman. He looked at the farmer and saw that the man was truly apprehensive. His larynx moved jerkily up and down. He apparently held this attitude about strangers foremost in his order of things, but why then had he stopped? Beckman felt ashamed at being a living part of the man's fear, but an answer to the question was expected. He wondered for a moment what the man would do if he said yes.

"Of course not." Beckman made it sound serious and slightly defensive.

The farmer exhaled a long breath of relief. "Where 'bouts you going?"

"Which way are you headed?"

"I'm going to Selby to sell them hogs."

"Which way is that?"

"Well, it's down this road 'bout ten mile, then down 142 for another five."

"Yes, but which way? What direction: north, south, east or west?"

"Why, west. At least until 142, then south to Selby. That whor you're going, to Selby?"

"No, I think. I'll go west. Maybe to California."

"Cal-i-for-ni-a," the farmer repeated slowly, biting his bottom lip. "Now that's a long way off. Never been there. Fact is, I've never been west of the mountains and don't know if I want to."

"The Rocky Mountains?" Beckman asked. The very sound of it unexpectedly thrilled him.

"No. The Appalachian, the Smokies, and I only saw them from afar. Never really cared much for going places." The farmer looked over at Beckman with a smile.

Beckman looked down the road. A surge of nausea and confusion passed through him. It truly seemed like the "road to nowhere". Wasn't that the title of a movie? Nowhere seemed to offer the best choice, the greatest shroud of protection.

He started to walk. He didn't want to hitchhike anymore. He wanted to walk to California. That would be his new fulfilling ambition, something approaching impossibility, but not "the impossible". That would be his new, higher goal, motivating him through all the grim drudgery, the peaks and valleys along the way. He would make his "road to nowhere" mean something.

He walked all that morning, occasionally tripping over objects hidden in the grass. He looked up at a large winged bird circling overhead and slipped off the shoulder, tumbling down a five-foot slope. He was uninjured, but wiser. His first big lesson—look where you're walking. Every foot of road ahead would have to be scanned, judged, and decided upon. He would know the road taken; every blade of grass, every crack in the highway, every bit of roadside trash. He would know his road the way a lover knows the body of his beloved.

Beckman climbed back up the slope and stood next to the highway feeling perversely proud of himself. He'd had his first tempering blow, and he felt now that he would accept anything nature could deliver. The gravity of this thought, the direct and, admittedly, pompous challenge to nature immobilized him for a while. It wasn't immobilization from fear but more of dimension, his mind trying to grasp the meaning of his new self, and his situation. He wondered, too, if it might not be a prelude to death, the romantic images of an explorer freezing to death but shaking his fist at the blizzard.

Could it be one of fate's last tricks on a desperate man, lulling him into the peace of indifference before closing the doors? Beckman reached down and picked up a piece of broken glass. He dragged the pointed edge across the top of his forearm. The cut wasn't deep. There was some blood, but the pain was not the same. It was only physical pain, biological, curable. It was not the pain that had been with him most of his life. That pain had been a living being, without form or visible cause but, nevertheless, a constant companion. One that he had come to rely on, a stable reference when all else was undefinable. Now it seemed to be gone, or at least left behind. He had been propelled into a different region of emotional space; foreign, but not threatening. Walking to California, something few pilgrims had done, was his destiny.

Beckman started to walk again; one part of his mind concentrating on the ground, the physical requirements of walking, the rest, racing toward some critical limit. Was he going insane? Was he walking into the world of endless distortions along the fusion line of mind and matter?

A car passed, blasting him with a concussion wave of hot air and scattering his hair like a madman of the desert. Had he slipped over into the prophetic ability to conclude without logical reasoning? It had happened to other casualties. Some had been friends of his. They had been thinkers then; wading in doubt, mystified by unfounded meanings, searching for and horrified at reality. He would see them later; clear-eyed, a beatific expression lighting their faces, and expounding opinions with undoubted conviction. "Just believe and be happy." This behavior seemed to happen so often that at times it seemed like a contagious disease. Had he picked up this disease somewhere along the road? Was he soon to start raving like some off-Broadway prophet?

He brushed his hair back into place. Malany had been right during one of their sleepy talks in bed. It was the destructive dichotomy—Malany's favorite word—of today's world that was terminating twentieth century mankind. It was insidious and incurable unless you were armed. Beckman realized, at that moment, that Malany was the only person he knew who was armed.

He stopped again. This time he heard something familiar, as familiar as Malany's voice. He turned and saw the diminutive face of Malany's car growing larger and roaring louder. The car was beside him before he had time to sort out his feelings. Noisily, beating rhythmically, it gave off the tremendous heat of an old beast determined to live, defying extinction. Malany leaned over to the passenger's window. Beckman was thrilled at seeing her long, angular face and her dark, fluid eyes that, in weaker moments, he had dreamed of loving.

She said, "Where are you going?"

"West," Beckman replied. "West."

"I thought so. Get in."

"I want to walk," Beckman said, shocked at the betrayal in his own voice.

"Nonsense. Get in."

Beckman opened the door, hesitated while his mind said good-bye to the private world he had known, and got in. They rode for a while in silence, Beckman readjusting himself to the world of Malany.

"How did you know where to find me?" he asked, genuinely puzzled.

"I resorted to your psychokinesis." She waited for this to take effect. "I simply allowed my mind to seek you out. It was like switching on an energy field and probing with high-sensitive electromagnetic feelings. Then, just like poetic inspiration, I knew where you were. I couldn't actually see you, of course. There wasn't an image. It was just that I knew where you were. I never doubted it."

"Why did you come?" Beckman asked.

"I had an intense feeling that we weren't finished."

"What if I think we are?" Beckman snapped.

"Are we?"

"Could it also have something to do with this being the only paved road going west out of town?"

"Don't be cynical, Beckman. I will not acknowledge it."

Beckman wanted to shout, "Yes!" The word erupted in his throat but dissipated before he could say it. He wanted to believe what she said, but conviction wasn't there. Abruptly he switched on the car radio, tuned to a rock music station.

"Please, would you turn that off? It's become tiresomely repetitious and conventional."

Beckman switched the radio off. "What happened back there?" he asked.

"Nothing unpredictable, I'm afraid. The timing was too distorted. I realized after you left that he was at the end of something and that I was at the beginning. Call it what you want. I've reached a point where I wish to only interpret life poetically, and he can only interpret it allegorically.

"You see, he thought that since I lived on the periphery of society and he had been cast out, that we automatically had something in common. This, of course, is true, but his motivation was all wrong. He believed that this situation allowed him the questionable luxury, and I know you don't agree, of emotional interaction, sex—that sort of thing. I wanted it to be strictly platonic; me the poetess, him the book dealer. I thought perhaps his bookstore could become an arts center. I know it sounds like gross self-indulgence but after that scene at the reading, I felt determined to prove myself.

"Anyway, he started the bit about being in love with me, wanting to have sex with me. I told him that I don't have sex, but he begged me, crying like a child, begging me to masturbate him. I consented just so he would stop screaming. It was a disaster. His withered little organ would do nothing. It looked like a dried worm. Finally, when I was afraid that it would start bleeding, he rushed out of the store, naked from the waist down, and tried to run his wheelchair head-on into the street traffic. I realized that I had made a mistake, so I drove to the motel to find you. And you know the rest."

"But Malany, why me? I was just beginning to make it on my own again. It was all beginning to make sense. I don't need you."

"Yes, you do, Beckman. We need each other. I can admit that now."

"Yes, I know. My con artistry and your literary artistry."

"Beckman, you're oversimplifying again."

"Just being allegorical."

"I concede. Let's just agree that it would be safer if we go west together. The people here are not yet ready for my work. It's a mad, primitive, and receptive world out there in the West and, after what's happened, I feel acutely vulnerable. I'm sure it's only a temporary negation. It has to be, or I'll never write again."

"Is that why you're going west?"

"Partly that, and partly to find "That New World." A poet who has shaken off tradition and its solidifying restrictions no longer needs all that stuff about stability, sitting before the fireplace surrounded by an adoring family. To me it has become the seal of death, like when the paraplegic started his muddle about finding someone and love and all that. I would just as soon be told that I had terminal cancer."

"Suppose when we get to where we're going, we find nothing but the Pacific Ocean. What then? Take the first boat going west? Jump off the Golden Gate Bridge? Isn't that an ironic name for one of the most popular suicide spots in the world?"

"Regardless of what we find, I don't think it will be the smug complacency of the east. Almost anything's better than that."

"Even death, Malany?"

"Beckman, anyone who has descended into contentment and complacency is dead. Only the true artist lives."

"Now who's oversimplifying?"

They came to an intersection made more significant by the presence of a gas station and convenience store. Malany stopped at the intersection, looked both ways for traffic, then impulsively pulled into the gas station.

"We need gas?" Beckman asked, looking over at the fuel gauge.

"I want to exemplify what I mean," Malany said.

The attendant walked toward the car, wiping his hands on an oily orange rag, and framed his weathered face in the opened window.

"Yes, ma'am?"

"Fill it up, please," Malany said. She smiled unaccustomedly at the attendant. Then, reaching across Beckman, opened the glove compartment and searched its small, cluttered chamber until she found a pencil and an old pad of paper. The attendant returned after a few moments.

"Didn't take much, ma'am. Be anything else?"

"Yes. I'm doing a survey for a possible television program on occupations in America, and if you don't object, I'd like to ask you some questions."

The attendant glanced at his watch, wrinkled his forehead.

"It won't take long," Malany assured him.

"All right, what would you like to know?"

"First of all, do you own your own business?"

"Yes ma'am, as much as anyone can own anything who has to live on borr'ed money."

"Any other means of income?"

"Little land under cultivation."

"Married?"

"Yes."

"Children?"

"Two boys."

Malany wrote the answers on the pad.

"Do you have a cemetery lot?"

"Not yet. Thought I would let that take care of itself someday." The attendant looked to one side. "You say this is for television?"

"Yes, a national survey."

"To tell you the truth, I don't watch it much."

"Okay, when you do watch it what types of programs do you like?"

"Oh, not much of anything. I seldom ever watch anything other than the news, maybe a baseball game now and then."

"Are you a subscriber to a book club?"

The attendant shook his head. "Nope, can't remember when I read a book last."

"Do you go to art shows?"

"Nope."

"Would you say that you are satisfied with your occupation?"

"That's an awful strange question, ma'am, but I guess television is a strange business. But to answer your question, I'd have to say yes."

"Thank you very much. You've been a great help." Malany put the pad and pencil back into the glove compartment and shifted into low gear.

"The gas was $2, ma'am," the attendant said. He was still framed in the window. Malany apologized, reached into her white envelope and withdrew a $5 bill. The attendant went back into the station and returned in a few minutes with her change.

"Are you convinced?" Malany asked.

"No," said Beckman. "The man seemed to be alive to me. He had a sense of humor. He has obviously made some decisions about his life within the restrictions he found himself. He's chosen honesty over criminality. He's made some decisions about death. He has some pride and dignity. Yes, I'd say he's very much alive."

"Oh, Beckman, you've missed the point. Don't you see? He'll never be anything else because he's satisfied with what he is. It's as final as death, never changes. It's the difference between art and non-art. Art and real life are always changing, always evolving, never satisfied with current truths. Non-art and death put an end to all of that. Death is the ultimate satisfaction. Can't you see that, Beckman?"

"He didn't sound exactly satisfied to me. I would say it was more like acceptance."

"That's even worse, Beckman. That's defeat."

"Oh bullshit, Malany. That sounds like the gratuitous logic of some art professor who has a steady job, a full stomach, and a real home to go to. The artist is no more important than any other creator. Can you really say that Bach was more important than Isaac Newton, or that Picasso knew more about truth than Einstein? In fact, and I know I risk being struck dead, I'm beginning to question the value of the artist anyway. After all, who really makes the world what it is? The artist? Or people like that gas station attendant or farmers or doctors who actually make things happen? What the hell can the artist do but present his version of what he thinks the world is and hope somebody with money will buy it? If nobody buys what we do, Malany, can we call ourselves artists?"

"That's convoluted logic, Beckman, and simply not true. Commercial success doesn't determine what art is or who is an artist. Art doesn't need sales to be art. It's terribly naive of you to even think so and, I must say, I'm surprised."

"I was merely . . ."

"Beckman!" Malany interrupted. "I'm not going to discuss it with you as long as you're in this adversarial mood."

Beckman knew that he had angered her and at once regretted it, but he didn't feel like apologizing or much like talking. His dream of walking to California was ruined. No sooner had he made the vow than he broke it. Almost the moment he decided on a new life, he slipped back into the old. He was bogged down in a thick glue of guilt and self-hate, and he wanted to sleep.

When he awoke, it was to the last desperate cry of someone calling his name. But it had been only the remnant of a dream, one that he could not remember. Or was it the sounds he continued to hear mixing above his head in the yellow, man-made light of the car windows? He started to sit up but hit his head on the steering wheel. Slowly he realized that he was lying on the front seat, head under the steering wheel. Malany was gone. He slipped his head past the wheel on the second try and sat up.

The car was in the parking lot of a Holiday Inn, under a sputtering light. The form of Malany sleeping in the back seat was illuminated in an electronic orange. Beckman was thirsty, he had to urinate, and he was lost. "Lost" reverberated back through his memory. All of his orientations of time and place were gone. He didn't know where he was nor what time it was. He felt like a small planetary body suddenly propelled away from a universe he had known, to spin alone forever.

This electronically lit parking lot, half-filled with strange vehicles, and the contemporary church-like form of the Holiday Inn motel were his universe, all suspended in night. Being lost, to Beckman, was not simple disorientation. It was continued existence continued. Life after death, and he didn't know what made him think of that. Was existence continued without meaning or purpose? If there was life after death, then it must be like being eternally lost. Beckman stepped out of the car quietly, gently closing the door. After checking to see if Malany was still asleep, he walked across the parking lot to the main entrance of the motel. There were no shadows in the main lobby. Everything—furniture, walls, doors, carpets—was all shadowless and seemed to come together without visible connections. The white light hurt Beckman's eyes and he stopped, for a moment, just inside the door while his eyes made the adjustment. He smiled at the motel desk clerk who, rigid as a steel sculpture, watched him, rotating his head and body as a unit to follow Beckman with his eyes as he walked past on his way to the men's room. Beckman stood over the urinal and thought about Henry Miller, and how right he had been to praise the pure joy and freedom of unrestrained urination. Is that what Herschel was experiencing? One look in the mirror, and he sympathized with the desk clerk. The past twelve hours had turned his jaw into a dark, prickly cactus. His clothes bore the stains and tears of his fall down the shoulder of the road. His hair lay piled and bunched on one side of his head. Beckman looked at his image in the mirror. He was who he should have been; he was recognizable. It was the other, the boy in the lobby, who was the alien and frightened. Beckman filled a sink with hot water. He studied his grotesque image for a long moment, not really displeased with it.

He washed his face and arms in the sink, and wiped as many of the stains as he could from his clothes. His teeth felt caked with a soft, fuzzy slime. That would have to wait. He brushed his hair back into uniformity, walked out to the water fountain, gulped as much water as he could hold and left, smiling again at the desk clerk on his way out. There was no security guard paid to smite the wrongdoer, no nervous management ushering him out, only the intemperate light and the strange quiet of the carpeted floor.

Outside, Beckman found himself in a group of people, all in evening clothes. They had been to a formal occasion and seemed unusually subdued for a group that large. They moved, en masse, out to the parking lot and Beckman moved with them, intrigued by their reticence and expressions of sadness. None of them seemed to notice Beckman. They were as cognizant of his presence as they would have been of an invisible spirit. Beckman even briefly wondered if he might have died somewhere in the motel lobby, possibly shot by the security guard he did not see, and this was to be his life after death.

Then, as though obeying a pre-arranged but inaudible, invisible signal, the group dispersed. Couples moved in all directions away from him to be absorbed into the vastness of the parking lot. He stood alone for a moment, thinking about this unexpected encounter with his formally dressed, unknown guests of an unknown function and realizing also that he still did not know what time it was or where he was. He thought of going back into the motel lobby to ask the desk clerk but no, that would not do. He did not even look back at the motel for fear that it, too, might have vanished.

Beckman walked to the car, almost at a trot. Malany was still asleep in the back. The keys, fortuitously, were in the ignition. He followed the motel driveway to where it intersected with a highway. There was the night glow of a town to his right and darkness to his left. Beckman turned left and, at the next intersection, stopped to read the road sign: *I-42 East*. Beckman turned left again and held the accelerator down past the speed limit, past the safe limits of the machine, toward the final, terminal end of gravity's ability to hold him. The road had become a lighted blur leading them further into the night and pointed directly toward the stars. Beckman hoped, even prayed, that at the right moment they would find themselves in space; insular, self-contained, a small, safe world all to themselves. Just at the moment when he thought it could happen, Malany started pounding on his head.

"Good God, are you trying to kill us? Have you flipped? Slow down!"

Beckman took his foot off the accelerator pedal. He was frightened. Some other force between matter and energy had almost taken him over, had almost drawn him through its bright, translucent screen. The horror of it became recognizable, and he apologized with tears in his eyes.

Malany settled back, and her breathing slowed down as she drifted back into sleep. When he was sure she was sound asleep, he switched on the radio. He didn't want to be alone with his mind or with the car, which sometimes seemed to be aware of its particular existence. An all-night preacher was shouting power and redemption in a voice imitating the crashing of cymbals and pounding drums. Beckman thought of him, sitting in an atmospherically controlled radio studio; well dressed, well fed, screaming his carefully timed code words linked with the appropriate Bible quotations, into the night. It was a powerful station too, coming loud and clear from somewhere in Oklahoma, rebounding around the world, offering to fill unbearable voids, or supply that immutable but illusive world of safety and predictability. A world market of the needy and vulnerable. What special immunity did the sellers have? Wasn't it true that the sellers never bought their own product? He thought of an encyclopedia salesman he once worked for who never owned a book, or the used car salesman who only rode the bus, or the pushers and frigid whores he had known; none of whom created or loved the things they sold.

The question was, Beckman thought, was it ever possible to give up, completely, ownership of something created and loved? If Malany sold her poems, they would still be her poems. No one could ever truly transmute their name onto them. They would always be hers. Then Beckman understood why his mother had taken such great pleasure in stories of fallen virtue. The married preacher discovered in bed with the spinster organist were her favorites. She needed the thrilling reassurance that the sellers of goodness were no better than the sellers of guns or drugs or flesh.

Thinking of his mother had always depressed him, often to the point of memory-destroying drunkenness or physical immobility. Thinking of her came like a sickness at times; with early symptoms of headaches, feverishness, and irritability, followed by loss of appetite, concluding in fatigue and days of incapacitation. He would not allow himself to get sick this time. He was on the move, going to California, a land full of sun and wonderfully out-of-joint people.

# CHAPTER 10

It was growing lighter outside, and the character of the land was beginning to change. Ahead, he saw the bottom teeth of a dead carnivore, the jagged line of the first Appalachian range, capped in glowing orange light. Malany crawled over from the back seat.

"Aren't they beautiful?" she said.

"Would you like to drive?" Beckman asked.

Malany looked offended. "Certainly not. I need to absorb all this magnificence." Beckman made a profane noise.

"You don't like the mountains?"

"No." he said.

"I can't believe it. Even someone like you must be impressed by them."

"I'm not."

"Why not? Do you have an intelligent reason?"

Beckman waited. "They are a barrier, like the ocean or a hymen. I don't like barriers. They are not challenges but really negative forces that try to limit you before you reach your natural limits. Why should anyone like what they have to struggle against? Barriers are threats, potential killers."

They had started to climb. The road was now divided into two lanes for the climbers and one lane for those coming down. Trees blocked out the mountains but occasionally, through narrow gaps, Malany could see fragments of blue sky below. The engine continually whined under the strain of the climb, and their middle ears swelled and popped periodically. Beckman swerved several times into the passing lane to avoid the probable path of a suspiciously loose overhanging rock. Other cars, more powerful, with learned drivers, passed him with what he thought was incredible speed.

They reached a turn where the trees had been cleared away and the pavement widened into a graveled pull-off area. A wooden sign identified the place as an "overlook". Beckman stopped the car and set the parking brake, a meaningless but necessary gesture, since he knew it would not work. Malany got out and walked toward the pipe railing erected around the entire area. Her black dress flowed like a misshapen flag. Beckman kicked a large stone behind the rear wheel, just in case. A sports car roared into the overlook and came to a sliding stop. Beckman noticed a college parking sticker on the bumper. He watched, intrigued, as the two Joe and Jane college types walked to the rail. The boy leaned against it, trusting it completely, and pulled the girl to him. They spoke in whispers with touching lips, steam rising from their mouths in puffing clouds. The boy pumped and squeezed the girl's buttocks with increasing frequency; both totally indifferent to the thousand-foot sheer drop only a foot away. Indifferent also to the checkered valley and sloping mountain behind them, the clear air, the painfully blue sky.

Malany never once pretended to notice the young lovers. She was too absorbed in the scene. She breathed in the cold mountain air like an anoxia patient on oxygen. The couple turned to glance at the scene, then indulged in another period of fondling before they walked back to their car and left.

Something of Beckman went with them, drawn from him in a painful extraction of unwilling breath. He looked around at the mountain and valley, and it was a harsh and primitive sight, alien and devoid of humanity.

"Are you ready to go?" he asked Malany.

"Beckman, you mean you could leave this? How cloddish can you be? I could spend the rest of my life here."

Beckman shrugged and walked toward the highway. Malany waited until he assumed the posture of a determined hitchhiker.

"All right," she said. "I hate it. Did you hear? I hate it, Beckman, stop! You ingrate, you intolerant bastard!"

Malany ran toward the car, lifting her black dress to knee length. Beckman didn't like playing games with her. He really wanted, genuinely wanted, to go, to make it to California alone if necessary, but he didn't want to be responsible for her injuring herself. He heard the car start and half turned to see it coming straight for him. Malany was behind the wheel, her face twisted with rage.

There was nowhere for him to go. A jump to the left would send him over the edge of the mountain. Jumping right would require two long steps to clear the car. And by the time he considered it, it was already too late—the car was too close. Malany stomped on the brakes a few feet from him. Beckman heard the force of it, like the deep sound of a fifty-gallon metal drum dropped on end. The car slid on all four wheels to within a foot of him. It was a moment or two before Beckman realized that he had been holding his breath and that, despite his will to move, paralysis had solidified his body.

"Beckman!" Malany shrieked from her opened window. "Beckman, get in. We're going together, Beckman, do you hear? We're going together!"

When Beckman was able to control his legs, he started moving away from the front of the car as cautiously as if it were a predator ready to strike.

"Only if you let me drive out of these hideous mountains."

The car leapt forward a couple of inches. Beckman stepped back until his heels were dangling over the edge of a rock.

"All right, goddamn it!" Her lips continued to move behind the windshield. She jerked on the parking brake. The car rolled forward another inch, just touching Beckman's pants.

Carefully avoiding a look backward and fearing that some

unknown force might yet draw him over the edge, Beckman slid around the body of the Oldsmobile to the driver's side. He looked at the empty space where he had defied the force of Malany's madness. There he saw parts of sky and the tops of trees sloping down. His mental vision had been right. The image he saw in his mind was what he saw before him now. He glanced over at Malany and at her black clad form, knotted in rage, her face streaked with craziness. He backed the Oldsmobile away from the ledge and out onto the road.

"Malany," he said. "Please don't speak for the next twenty-four hours."

Beckman shrugged and started the long, low gear coast down the mountain. He was feeling irrationally guilty and was angry with himself for feeling this way. It was pointless, meaningless. Malany had set the rules from the very first, and when the plans failed, theoretically the rules no longer applied. Yet she had hunted him down and, after choosing the paraplegic, now insisted on Beckman's company to the point of murder. Beckman wasn't sure that his reasons for going with her now were not simply fear for his life, or that he was still drawn to the dark figure of Malany; her strange, convoluted mentality, her private orbit of mystery.

He continued to drive until they were out of the mountains and into the foothills of Tennessee. It was almost dark, the fuel was low, and Beckman was beginning to feel sleepy. He passed a sign establishing Knoxville as forty miles away. He would never make that, so he began looking for a suitable place to park the car. Malany had moved to the back seat an hour ago and had lost herself in her book of poetry.

Several miles ahead, Beckman saw a group of buildings that seemed to have merged into one. A painted sign, lit by flashing lights, advertised MOTEL, GAS, EATS, BEER & BILLIARDS. He pulled into the gas station part, filled the tank, and drove the next hundred feet to the motel part.

"I know what you said," Beckman told Malany, "but I'm going to tell you this. I want a decent night's sleep on clean sheets. I want to wash the grunge off my body, and I need to eat something."

Malany glared at him with two black pits for eyes.

"I need some money, Malany. You always have money. God knows where you get it. I've been wanting to ask you about that anyway. Where do you get the money you keep in that envelope?"

Malany handed over a roll of bills. Beckman counted out what he thought the room might cost, and enough for a truck stop meal.

Beckman took a long hot shower, dug out a change of underwear from his bag, tried to shave with a month-old razor blade, looked at his stubble for a long time and decided to let it grow if it didn't come out red. Malany was lying on the bed reading her poetry book, ignoring him.

"I'll be back in about an hour."

Malany gave no indication that she had heard him.

In the EATS section of the building, Beckman found an empty table.

Sitting at the counter had always seemed a little like eating at a trough. He ordered the chopped steak special and waited, listening to the truck drivers at the next table talk of "smokes," radar detection devices, speed limits, and "gov'ment" interference in their "bid'nes."

The place was lit in brilliant white fluorescent light. Every flaw, every chipped plate and wedge of dirt was clearly exposed. The outside was completely blotted out except for occasional truck lights passing across the large window. The cracking voice of a female country singer, wailing about adultery and divorce, filled the terrible spaces between live human sounds.

Beckman finished the gravy-smothered meal, paid for it, and

eased by two highway punch-drunk truckers swallowing coffee and uppers. He wasn't anxious to go back to the room and sit in the heat of Malany's fury. What was she angry about anyway? Because he hit the road? Beckman was genuinely afraid Malany might actually kill him next time. Also, she needed him—or rather, she had not needed him when they first met.

He stopped under the neon sign to the billiards room, a flashing red arrow shot down toward the door. Beckman could hear the jarring clash of the hard balls hitting together with enough force, it seemed, to break apart, although he had never actually known of one breaking. The thought seemed never to be considered by players. Were the balls truly indestructible? Did anyone care?

He went in, intending to waste a couple of hours—enough time for Malany to fall asleep—and took the first available seat next to one of the tables. One of the players, a leather-jacketed man between twenty and forty with a winged Harley Davidson patch over his left pocket and a half-burned cigar in one side of his mouth, eyed his opponent's shooting. Beckman guessed they were locals out for a big night. The opponent bit his lips and concentrated on the shot. It was a difficult one, the number four ball in the corner pocket. The shot would have to go between two balls and bank off the side at the proper angle to make it. The opponent sighted the path with his cue stick, shook his head.

"Aw hell, boy. Go ahead and shoot. It's only a Lincoln."

The opponent wasn't going to be rushed. He walked slowly around the table, looking at the shot from all promising angles, then readied himself, leaning over the shooting side and taking practice jabs at the cue ball. Then, with an orgasmic release, struck the cue ball. The ball shot cleanly between the two obstacles, bounced off the side with decreasing speed, and rolled straight toward the four ball. The players, and Beckman, watched intently as the cue ball tapped the four ball with just the right amount of force to send it rolling toward the pocket. The opponent had begun to smile, but something happened. The four ball seemed to wobble. It touched the tip of the pocket's corner, where it spun to a stop on the rim of the hole.

"Son of a bitch," the opponent breathed without passion, as though the very breath he had used to utter his tragic surprise was knowingly useless. The man in the leather jacket grinned joyously at his shift in fortune. He shoved his cigar in the other corner of his mouth and triumphantly began chalking his cue tip.

"I 'preciate you settin' me up like that, Slim," he said with a slight smile.

Although Slim, remembering that it was "just a game," tried to smile, he was a man who had been given a sentence of execution. The man in the black leather jacket, called "Hoss" by his opponent, leapt back into the game, swung his cue stick like a sword, and tapped the four ball with enough English to send the cue ball swirling into position for the five ball. Hoss sank seven balls all the way up to twelve, each ostensibly done with the irreverent carelessness of a man used to good luck. When it came down to the actual execution, that is, actually going through with a shot, Beckman noticed the intensity of Hoss's concentration. He felt sure Hoss had psychokinetic ability, but how developed was it? Hoss's opponent went after the next shot like a man resigned to suicide, and missed.

"Oh shit."

The partner kicked the floor with his heel, then punished the cue stick with a hard slap of his hand. He was finished, the game was decided. He reached into his jeans pocket, brought up what was probably the last bill he had (it was a Lincoln), and tossed it toward the table where it floated to a soft landing next to the cue ball. Hoss grinned and watched as the money drifted down.

"Aw, come on, boy. At least finish the game."

But his opponent had already racked his cue stick and was loping, hunched and small, toward the door. Hoss shrugged and laid his cigar on the edge of the pool table. He began, as methodically as an assassin, to sink the remaining balls. Beckman remained, matching the final exhibition of skill, acknowledging with a nod the successful completion of difficult shots which, by now, he was convinced took more than simple manual dexterity.

Hoss was aware of Beckman's presence and his interest in the game. He waited until he was sure of Beckman's riveted attention before making what he considered a "good" shot. When the last ball had dropped into the pocket, Hoss stood up next to the table, surveyed the empty green field, and calmly chalked his cue stick. He looked over at Beckman and signaled with his finger.

Beckman, crouching on his high stool, leapt down like a bird and, straightening himself to homo-erectus form, went to where he was being summoned. Hoss would not play for less than $5 a game. It took that, he said, to sharpen the competitive edge and help him concentrate. Beckman, although he had spent many hours watching other people play, had never actually played the game himself.

He knew the rules, the scores, the terminology, but not how to put his spirit into the cue stick. How could he make a wooden cue stick become a living part of his mind and body? This he would have to learn. Yet wasn't this even closer to the practice of psychokinesis than what he had to do at the restaurant where he had been at the mercy of Herschel's foul penis and the primitive derangement of his boss?

Here, on the pool table, he could be in control. He could move the balls anywhere he wanted. If he was strong enough, the most he could hope for was total command or, at least, a draw. He couldn't lose.

Hoss racked the balls into a neat triangle. He shook the triangle several times until the balls made a concordant rap. He then rolled the triangle of balls to the center of the table, placing the tip on the spot, then deftly removed the varnished wooden form without the slightest disturbance to the balls.

Hoss smiled, put his cigar back in the preset corner of his mouth, dug around in his jacket pocket, then flipped a nickel into the air, catching it in one hand and slapping it on his leathered wrist. Beckman, to his surprise, won the toss and positioned himself for the break.

He lined the cue ball up directly with the point ball. Unfortunately, his psychokinetic energy would be dispersed and, for any decided purpose, would be useless. The best he could do would be to concentrate on the cue ball as he had watched Hoss do, and rely on the statistical probability of one of the balls going in. He thought about it, sighting down his cue stick. The chances on this shot were in the shooter's favor. He had witnessed only one break that did not put at least one ball in. He concentrated on the cue ball and the path it would travel to the point ball. He could see the point of impact on the triangle. Sheer force would make the difference, the wonderful, living energy only he could deliver.

The cue ball seemed to swell twice its original size and grow as dense as lead. Beckman concentrated until his face felt hot and his temples throbbed. Everything would have to be delivered by the tip of the cue stick to a point slightly above center on the cue ball. He heard himself grunt as the cue stick traveled, burning through his hand to its target. There was a "crack" like the sound of rocks breaking. The triangle exploded into a mad spectacle of ricocheting, colliding balls. Beckman counted three dropping in almost immediately. The remainder rolled to positions all over the table.

"Hot damn!" Hoss said. "Sh-e-e-e-it!"

Beckman studied the table. He was lined up for a deflection shot on the one ball. Not a bad situation, really, but to be effective he would have to hit the cue ball so that it would not only sink the target ball but roll in a straight line to the left for a position on the two ball. Control of the cue ball was now most important. If he could sustain his energy, he could "run" the game.

Beckman sank the two ball, but his concentration was diverted for a moment toward the two ball when it touched a corner of the pocket. The cue ball rolled short of its desired position so that to make a success out of it, Beckman would have to bank the shot thirty degrees off the side. He concentrated on the cue ball until sweat started to form on his hands and face. He even reached up and wiped his brow to see if he was actually sweating blood. The sweat that he had thought stood out like thorny beads on his forehead showed up as a dirty smear on his fingers. He lay over the table sighting the shot, hands out spread like an oriental supplicant. And then, what he had hoped for happened.

The cue ball seemed to pulsate like a pre-Nova star. Its surface seemed to flow in swirls of molten plastic lava. A part of Beckman's consciousness seemed to leave his mind and enter the excited cue ball. That part of his mind wandered through the soulless interior of the ball, caressing every plastic molecule of its structure, infusing them with independent life. Beckman, in his mind, saw what was going on inside the cue ball. He could see the clear, rounded globs of complex polymer chains all interconnected in an elastic high-strength configuration. He was paralyzed by this vision until the voice of Hoss shattered it into exploding bits of color.

"This boy's a hustler, Louis. He's trying to make me sweat. Go ahead, boy, shoot. It's only $5."

Beckman shot, but the instant the stick connected with the cue ball he knew he had missed it. The cue ball banked at the right angle, tapped the three ball, which rolled toward the pocket but stopped short. Hoss grinned, then lit another cigar, bouncing it up and down between his teeth.

"Louis, bring us a couple of beers, will you?" He looked directly at Beckman. "You'd like a beer, wouldn't you, boy?"

"No thanks."

Hoss shrugged. "Well, I ain't often that generous, but it don't matter. I'll drink it myself."

The bartender brought two mugs of beer and sat them on a stool near Hoss. He held a mug of beer and cigar in one hand and gulped the other beer with the other hand. Beckman counted five seconds before the contents of the glass vanished. Hoss lowered the mug slowly. His chin was covered with foamy streaks. He wiped his mouth and chin with the palm of his hand and placed everything, including his cigar, on a small shelf next to the wall.

The one house rule, posted everywhere Beckman happened to look, forbade any article whatsoever from being placed on the tables. Hoss made the shot and sank the next two. Beckman made the next two. Hoss made one but missed the next one. The game went on like that, neck and neck; not so much a game of skill but more. Beckman firmly believed it was a contest of minds. He won the first match by a few points. Hoss reluctantly dropped his $5 onto the table, swilled his other beer, and demanded another match, insisting on it as a right of the loser.

The second game was played with even stronger intensity. Hoss put aside his cigar and jokes and fought with the tenacity and single-mindedness of a desperate man. The conflict soon drew the attention of other players in the pool room. Bets were taken, encouragements shouted to both players. Hoss won, but it was a close match that left him visibly shaken. Beckman asked for the best two out of three, but Hoss refused. Beckman's backers began threatening violence.

"All right, all right. But this is gonna be the last one. I ain't got time to fuck around here all night just so's you fellas can gamble."

"Bullshit, Hoss. I seen you play all night against someone you can beat," one of the bystanders said.

Hoss leapt toward the speaker, but was held back without much effort. He shouted over the heads of the spectators, "You just wait, you hear? Just wait till I'm finished."

Someone shoved a draft beer into Hoss's hand and he sipped it, watching with subsiding fury as Beckman readied himself for the break. The break was very successful with four drops, but Beckman had used up most of his vital energy in the last two games. He was counting on being able to keep Hoss out of step.

Halfway through the game, Beckman knew that he wasn't going to make it. He wasn't able to hold his concentration for more than a few minutes at a time. The green field of the table looked more faded and marked with uncountable burns. He excused himself while Hoss was preparing to make his decisive shot. He found a pay phone out of sight of the table and called Malany. She sounded conciliatory and redemptive. Beckman explained what had happened; that he didn't have $5 and that he didn't want her to pay for his mistakes.

Yes, she would do as he asked. "The motel is a rat's nest anyway," and the clientele frightened her. "Everyone looks like a rapist or axe murder," she said, and she was serious.

Beckman felt a surge of warmth toward Malany, something he had not felt since their first meeting in the bookstore. He had a sudden compulsion to say something good and kind and, yes, sentimental, but she had already hung up. For a moment, Beckman imagined her dashing around the room wonderfully nude, frantically preparing for their departure.

Beckman returned to the table and tried his best but, as he knew, it wasn't good enough. He was going under and fast. Those betting on him, however, were not disposed toward stoicism or even good sportsmanship. The most vocal condemned him as a phony, "a stupid fucking hippie." One even threatened him with the heavy end of a cue stick. Hoss found himself in the awkward position of defending his now-defeated opponent. He stepped in front of Beckman with renewed bravado, arms spread out, fist holding $20 bills. He ordered a round of beer for everybody. The crowd surged toward the bar.

"Now let's get out of here, boy." He took Beckman by the arm, past the momentarily diverted mob, and led him outside. Temporarily safe and among the lights and roar of diesel trucks, Hoss held out his hand and smiled.

"That's what I want to talk to you about," Beckman said, tapping the ground with his foot and feeling strangely sad that his shoe was covered with dust.

"I want to thank you for what you did in there." Beckman shook Hoss's extended hand in several spasmodic jerks.

"Never mind about that. Gimmee!" Hoss demanded.

"I have to go back to my room to get it."

Hoss looked toward the motel doubtfully. "Well, Hoss, I'll go with you just to see you don't forget about me along the way."

"Why did you call me Hoss?" Beckman asked.

"Hell, boy, everybody who's feared, mistrusted, or made fun of around here is called Hoss."

"Which are you, then?" Beckman asked.

"Me, I'm feared and mistrusted—least I hope so."

They walked past the car. Malany was behind the steering wheel, the engine was running, and Beckman thought that he noticed the passenger door cracked open. Hoss ignored Malany. It wasn't unusual for a woman to be waiting outside this motel with the engine running. Beckman pretended to have trouble with the room door.

"See what you can do, Hoss. Seems to be stuck."

Hoss grabbed the doorknob with both hands, twisted it, and threw his weight against it. The door burst open, tumbling Hoss inside. Beckman ran toward the car, leapt in, thankful that Malany had really left the door open, and locked it. The Oldsmobile jerked backward.

"Take it easy!" Beckman shouted.

Malany was overreacting. She had trouble shifting gears. Beckman looked back to see Hoss charging toward them, head lowered, legs and arms pumping. The car jerked forward, and there was the soft sound of flesh thudding against metal as Hoss pounced onto the back of the car.

Beckman turned around. He could see Hoss's silver western belt buckle, emblazoned with horseshoes and branding irons, pressed against the rear window. Hoss, Beckman imagined, was hanging on, spread eagle half across the roof and trunk, secured with tenuous finger and toe holds. Malany stopped abruptly at the highway to avoid being destroyed by an eighteen-wheeler, and Beckman watched as Hoss rolled, hunched like a wounded animal, onto the parking lot, his leather jacket flying open like clipped bat's wings. The truck passed, and Malany floored the accelerator, spraying dirt and rocks toward the motel's pool and gas sign. Beckman continued to look, fascinated at Hoss's determined pursuit. Hoss sprung up and ran after them, shaking both fists, his mouth screaming unheard curses.

The trusty Oldsmobile, hissing like a jet, continued to accelerate, carrying them to safety without missing a beat. Hoss was a small stick figure before he stopped running and began stomping the highway. Gone forever.

# CHAPTER 11

"Isn't it wonderful, Malany? Most people have to remain and deal with their mistakes, but you and I, we can experiment, we can play. No compromises for us, no bargaining, no apologies. No part of us left behind or given away. I'm beginning to see why the nomadic life is so appealing. Like my gifted teacher in American Lit. 302 who, from nine until three, would think nothing of inciting a riot, assaulting social values and attacking ancient mores all with eyes aflame and passionate. But let three o'clock come and he would straighten his tie and jacket, drive home to wifey and the kiddies and go shopping on Thursdays for supermarket bargains. Ah, Malany. It's truly California for us, where people, even third-generation natives, still keep the pioneer spirit alive by referring to continental travel as either 'out West' or 'back East'."

Malany nodded vigorously. "Yes, just as though everybody really belonged in the East."

They laughed, welcoming the easy calm following a successful escape—that warm ooze of wellbeing after the crisis has passed.

"But why did you do it, Beckman?" Malany asked.

"It was a good experimental situation. Control is nearly impossible in psychokinesis, so much depends on how you feel at the time. Predictably, I would be tuned up, so you can really see the effect of the mind over things, especially when a subject like Hoss is unaware of the experiment."

"Beckman, you make it all sound so sensible. I think you could even have me believing it."

"I'll swear, Malany, there is something to it, after all. Christ is supposed to have walked on water, you know. Every Christian is supposed to believe that, aren't they? If walking on water isn't the ultimate in psychokinesis, then what is? And what about all those miracles, all that healing of the sick and that last bit about ascending to Heaven? The Bible doesn't say anything about there being machines doing it, or mirrors."

Malany slowed down. The terrain was becoming hilly, and the road narrower and more curvaceous. Beckman saw a reflection in the windshield, a weak spot of light taking the curves behind them. He turned around and saw a single light beam approaching them, fast. The light had the jerky movements of a motorcycle. Beckman's first thought was that a policeman was on them, but motorcycle cops became extinct in most parts of the country fifteen years ago, and they had not been used on the open highway for longer than that.

The motorcycle stayed close behind, almost, it seemed, touching the bumper occasionally, and held this position until they reached a straight stretch in the road. Then it pulled abruptly over and started to pass. The cyclist came alongside the car and kicked Malany's door. The noise was sickening.

"It's that thug from the motel!" Malany shrieked.

Hoss kicked the door again, his mouth and throat working, but the wind carried away his angry words. Headlights appeared in the left lane and Hoss throttled back to his former position, a few inches from Malany's rear bumper. Malany sought deliverance in the accelerator pedal. Beckman shouted encouragement laced with panic. Malany was going to push the old, tired car once again to its physical limit.

A curve sign appeared, and then the curve. Malany took her foot abruptly off the pedal just before entering the curve. Beckman watched through the rear window. Hoss tried to make the right corrections. The motorcycle weaved several times, then seemed to wobble—more like a shudder.

It was far enough behind them now so that Beckman could no longer see the unified form of Hoss astride his motorcycle. The single headlight abruptly curved toward the road. A rooster tail of orange sparks rose from the highway. The headlight pointed skyward for a few long moments, waved its white finger several times, then went out. Malany skidded to a stop, and they both watched as the sparking machine launched itself over the hillside and became a meteoric red giant. Burning gasoline fell along its trajectory, lighting a path on the ground to where the motorcycle had come to rest, its tires burning in grotesque rings of fire.

"Don't get out!" Malany screamed.

But Beckman was already out of the car and staring down at the holocaust. He looked back up the road, and in the firelight saw a moving figure lying at the side of the road, near the edge of the drop-off.

When Beckman reached him, Hoss was propped up on his elbows, turning his head from side to side. Beckman could see that he was injured. His face had blood on it, his pants were ripped in shreds, and one leg was twisted under the other.

"Are you okay? How do you feel, Hoss?"

"Like I been chewed up and spit out. She-e-e-it!"

Hoss was looking toward the fire. "All that over $5. I can't believe it. I musta taken that curve a hundred times in the past year, without so much as a bump. I just can't believe it."

"You think you can move? Do you think a bone is broken?" Beckman asked.

Hoss looked down at his leg. "I don't think so. Check it out for me, would you?"

Beckman gently felt for swelling or an abnormal protrusion. "I don't feel anything, Hoss, but you still may have a small fracture."

Hoss began moving the leg, straightening it out. "There, that ain't so bad. Hurts a little bit. I don't think it's broken. Feels like I mostly skinned it up. God damn if I didn't ruin this jacket though, and it cost me nearly $70 too. Here, hep me up, boy."

Hoss extended his hand, which Beckman took with some reluctance, and he carefully pulled Hoss to his feet.

"Wh-e-e-e, that smarts! Feels like my buns have been shaved off and sanded smooth, boy, She-e-e-it!"

"That's good. If you can stand on it, that's good."

Hoss was looking toward the Nova's dying flames and the black, skeletal form of the motorcycle.

"I'm sorry about that. I had no idea that you were going to take it that seriously," Beckman said.

Malany had managed to turn the car around and was headed toward them.

"Yep." Hoss continued to look toward the flames, the yellow and red light dancing on his blood and dirt-smeared face. "Yep. It don't make no sense when you think about it."

"Is the cycle insured?"

"Nope. Couldn't afford it. Only had mine insured. That one belonged to my ex-wife. Wrecked mine just last week. Had to talk myself silly just to get her to let me use it tonight. She's not going to like this one bit."

Malany had stopped beside them and was shouting for Beckman to get in the car.

"Hoss, do you want us to take you to the hospital?" Beckman asked.

"Nope. I'm all right. You can drop me off in town, if you don't mind."

Hoss, with Beckman beside him, limped over to the car.

"How far is town?" Beckman said, noticing Malany's unaccustomed anxiety.

"'Bout ten miles."

"He's all right, Malany. Only bruised a little. He wants to be taken into town."

"Yes ma'am, I'd really 'preciate it."

"You know, if you have any ideas about calling the police, you'll be wasting your time," Malany said.

"Oh no, ma'am. I stay away from them people as much as I can. They're my natural enemy, just like cats and dogs—know what I mean?"

Malany nodded her consent, and Beckman helped Hoss into the back seat.

As they neared the town, Hoss slipped into silence and Beckman feared that he might have passed out.

"No, I'm feeling better all the time," Hoss answered. His voice did sound more vigorous, more like it had sounded in the pool room. "You know, I was just wondering where you boys were going."

"California," Malany answered sharply.

"I tell you what, I got $300 cash with me right now. You can have it all if you'll let me go along with you."

"What? Why?"

"Well, there's nothing for me here. My ex is gonna want to shoot my balls off when she hears about her motorcycle. If she don't do it, her boyfriend will, and, sooner or later, the cops are gonna nail me, guilty or innocent. They won't give a shit. Besides, there's just nothing here anymore but trouble. Damned if California don't sound like the place. How about it? You all could use $300, I know it."

"This may surprise you, Hoss, but we have enough money of our own. We don't need your petty bribes," Malany said.

"Come on. I can be a lot of hep with the driving and so on, and $300 ain't petty cash. Besides, you fellers look like you could use some protection."

"What kind of protection?" Malany asked.

"It can be an awful mean place out there, and you fellers can't always run. Sometimes you might not make it. You might have to stand and fight. That's where I can come in."

"To begin with, Hoss, I happen to be a woman."

"Yes ma'am, I can see that. But, you know, I only meant fellers as friendly, like we was all one family."

"Please, we don't need the protection you offer. We have found that one can avoid violence. The whole idea is repugnant to me."

"Malany, I really could have used him in that place back in Virginia, and we do need help with the driving, conventional as it may sound."

Malany nodded. "Yes, you're right, I suppose. But, my God, a few minutes ago he was trying to kill us."

"Well," Beckman said. "You see how quickly things can change, how ironic life really is. A few minutes ago, we were running for our lives. Now we've saved the very person who was pursuing us."

Malany stepped on the brakes, turned, and followed Hoss's finger to a Drug Mart.

"I want to go and get something to put on these scratches before they all turn to pus." Hoss limped boldly into the discount drugstore, ignoring two adolescent girls giggling at his condition.

"It's a mistake, Beckman, this redneck."

"Why do you say that, Malany? He's not much different from us."

"He's an ignorant brute who could turn on us at any moment."

"As I still say, he is not that much different from us."

"Oh, Beckman, there you go again, retreating back into that impervious shell of yours. You know perfectly well what I mean. What if it had worked out differently? What if he had not had that accident? How would you have felt about him then?"

"Malany, don't you think it's pointless to try to justify your prejudices, or whatever they are, on speculation?"

"I know the type, Beckman. I've spent my life observing people, and I warn you, again, that brute is a mistake, and your responsibility."

"Then what are you waiting for? You can simply back up and leave. It's your car, you're driving. You're making the decisions and, I might add, casting blame. I'll go along with whatever you decide, and I'll be quiet about it. But, whatever you decide, it makes you also responsible."

Malany flinched and groped at the gear shift lever, then jerked her face toward Beckman. "Oh, you're good at this verbal chess, aren't you, Beckman? If you were half as good a writer as you are at games, they would be handing you a gold-plated Pulitzer."

Hoss was returning, and the sight of him—ragged, dirty, bloody and limping—seemed to stun her. She trembled slightly as Hoss opened the car door and half fell into the back seat. "J-e-e-e-sus! I didn't realize I looked so bad. Must'a scared those little girls to death. Tell you what, though, just one more favor?"

Malany glared at Beckman.

"There's a do-it-yourself car wash place just down the road. If you'll pull in there for five minutes, I'll wash this shit off me, and we can get on to good old California smelling all nice and pretty."

"You'll have to admit it was a good idea," Beckman said as they watched Hoss, naked except for his undershorts, direct the nozzle of the car washing wand over his body. Then, Hoss, grinning like a naughty boy, gathered what was left of his clothes and ran toward the car.

"Oh, God. Look at him. He's several rungs lower on the evolutionary scale, a regressive mutant, and I'll bet he eats raw meat."

Hoss used one of Malany's two towels, jumped into the back seat, and began putting on his clothes.

"Hope you don't mind if I lay my undershorts out next to the window to dry."

Malany sighed angrily and started the car. She yanked the shift lever into drive and spun out onto the road. Hoss began to nod, then his head slumped forward.

"'Ott damn, ain't this great?" he said, reviving after a few minutes and shaking his head. "And it's only about five in the morning. By the way, where are we now? I must'a dozed off."

"About a hundred miles east of Memphis."

"That's just about right."

"Right for what?" Malany asked.

"I can't wear these all the way to California. We can find one of them military surplus stores and pick up some new threads."

"It'll have to be the Salvation Army."

"Not me, no sirree! Nobody goes to the Salvation Army but hippies and dirt—poor niggers."

Malany slammed on the brakes. The car immediately went into a skid, spinning around on the highway several times.

"Don't you ever use that word in front of me again, do you hear! Ever!"

"That word?" Hoss was bewildered and looked at Beckman.

"You know what 'that' word is. I can't stand it. I won't have it!" Malany shouted.

"God almighty! What word?" Again, Hoss looked toward Beckman.

"The one derogatory of black people, African Americans," Beckman explained in a calm voice.

"Oh, you mean . . ."

"Don't say it!" Malany screamed.

"All right, all right. Take it easy. I didn't mean nothing by it. What'd you call it?"

"Derogatory."

"Yeah, that's it. I didn't mean it that way, and even if I did, which I didn't, there's no need for us to continue sitting in the middle of the road."

"I want you to swear that you'll never use that word in my presence again."

"Now, wait a minute. I apologized, didn't I? Now, I think that's enough."

"Not for me, it isn't."

A car flashed by, horn blaring, a dusty vortex boiling up where the car had momentarily left the pavement.

"This is no place to discuss the race question," Beckman insisted.

Another car, coming from the opposite direction, swerved several times and, in a blast of blue-black smoke, roared around Malany's Oldsmobile, its driver glaring and gesticulating.

"That guy's going to call the cops," Beckman said.

"Did he have a C.B.?" Hoss asked, looking around at the departing car, now partially shielded by a screen of dust and smoke.

Malany, biting her lips pale, started off again. Hoss directed his attention to Beckman.

"Where'd you learn a word like you used back there?"

"Beckman thinks he's a writer, obsessed with words. He's drawn like Theseus into the labyrinth of their meanings. Right, Beckman?" Malany said.

"Please, Malany. He'll find out your position soon enough. Malany isn't completely right. I've tried to use words that way as a writer, and maybe I have gotten lost in a labyrinth or two, but I also try to create words whenever I have the chance. It's not easy." Beckman glanced at Malany. "And she also reads other people's books," he added. Malany flinched but said nothing.

"You been to college?" Hoss asked.

"I didn't finish," Beckman said.

"And you learned words like that?"

"Yes."

"Well, I'll be damned. I guess there's hope for all of us."

"I wouldn't go so far as to say that, Hass," Malany said, deliberately mispronouncing his name.

"How about you there . . . Malany. You been to college?"

Malany nodded.

"Well then, that explains it."

"Explains what?"

Silence.

"Ah, why you can use them words, and why you're so sure of yourself. College girls are always sure of themselves."

"Malany's a poet, Hoss," Beckman said.

"That so? Well, how about that? Don't read much poetry myself. In fact, haven't read anything since high school. But from what I remember, it must take a special kind of person. Know what I mean?"

"Her book is there beside you."

Hoss looked down. "This it?"

"Yes," Malany said.

Hoss surveyed the cover and squinted at the title on the front.

"Looks like somebody stepped on it."

"That happened at the last reading. The people were so anxious to get a copy that a few books were trampled in the rush," Beckman said.

"Damned if that don't sound like the way to live," Hoss said, opening the book, leafing through several pages, and stopping on a page in the middle of the book. He read the text with moving lips. His eyes moved slowly from word to word and occasionally searched for the next line. He closed the book and returned it to its corner of the car's floor.

"'Course I never did understand poetry. Round here, at least when I was a kid, if you were caught readin' that stuff you got called a fag. I never really believed that boys who read poetry were fags but, you know, some of them acted faggy; limp-wristed, that kind of thang. My heroes was Elvis, Jimmy Dean, all them fast-livers. You never heard of them reading poetry. Guess that was the trouble, huh? The wrong kind of heroes. Shit, I could'a been slinging big words around, maybe writing books myself."

"Don't feel bad, Hoss. Look where big words and college have gotten us," Beckman said.

"Hey, that's right!" Hoss laughed. "I'd be no further than I am now. But then again, I had a buddy back in the service. He went on the GI Bill—studied some kind of engineering. Now he's some kinda big shot over at Oak Ridge."

"The world always honors those who know its rules before it honors those who know its heart," Malany said.

"What does she mean by that?" Hoss asked.

"She means that people with practical knowledge are considered more valuable; that is, what they can do is considered more important than what the artist does."

"Well, that only makes sense, don't it?"

Malany looked away in disgust.

Hoss, seeing Malany's reaction, quickly added, "What I mean is, artists are important too. But people got to eat first, don't they? They got to clothe and shelter themselves, don't they?"

"That's all utter and complete nonsense, Mr. Hoss. It is a question of what people think they need."

"Damn, boy, if she don't talk crazy."

"She's a pure idealist, Hoss. You see, she's not supposed to care whether she eats or has a place to sleep or clothes to wear."

"No shit," Hoss said, genuinely amazed.

"It's not difficult to understand, Hoss, but really very difficult to put into practice as Malany has. It takes a special kind of person to do it."

"Yeah," Hoss said, looking at the back of Malany's head. "I can see that. Well, if she's one of them idealists, then what are you?" There was a demand in Hoss's tone; not an angry demand, but one of urgency.

"I don't know," Beckman said. "Sometimes I'm an idealist, other times I'm a materialist; but mostly, I simply don't know."

"Hey, boy, that's me," Hoss said, excited. "Only I don't know or give a damn all the time." He laughed and slapped the back of the seat. "It's the only way to be, ain't it?"

Beckman started to answer. He wanted to keep the conversation with Hoss rolling before it darted off into the rollicking, laughing, slap-happy nonsense chatter of the bored and misaligned. Before he could say anything, however, Hoss shouted for Malany to turn.

They had entered the heavier traffic of the city of Nashville long before, and Beckman had not been paying attention to the road signs. He had completely forgotten, as he was sure Malany had, that Hoss wanted to buy clothes. Malany veered the car onto an exit, with all the energy of a last, desperate act of self-preservation.

"Sorry to shake you up like that," Hoss apologized. "But the turnoff came up on me so fast that I didn't realize it. Damned if you ain't pretty good behind the wheel." Hoss patted her on the shoulder.

Malany recoiled as though she had been touched by hot metal. "Why on earth did you make me leave the interstate?" she asked.

"So I can go to the army-navy surplus store. You know, to buy some jeans. I can't go to California in these." He pointed to his clothes.

"You'll have to direct me. I'm lost."

"Don't worry, Malany. I know this town inside and out, just straight down this street for a few blocks, and you'll come to it."

Malany drove until the street terminated into a T intersection. "Hell, which way now?" she demanded.

"Now wait a minute. I know where I'm at, just wait a minute."

Hoss put his hand to his forehead like a priest seized with intense prayer. Then, with the assuredness of a professional conjurer, said, "Turn right."

Malany did as instructed, throwing impatient, angry glances at Beckman. Beckman felt, for the first time, that bringing Hoss along may have been a mistake; and that Hoss, like some jesting court fool, was leading them into an inextricable vat of humanity.

"Now turn left," Hoss said.

Malany did so at the moment the light changed to red. Halfway down the block and protruding slightly from the almost unbroken line of pawnshops, bargain stores, and porn shops, stood Lew's Armie Navie Store.

Malany parked the car under a large red, white, and blue sign done in the style of an American flag and bearing the warning *Absolutely No Personal Checks Cashed* and *This Property Protected by Smith and Wesson*.

Hoss jumped out and stretched his body. Beckman started to follow, but Malany caught him by the arm.

"Are you going in?" she whispered with such vehemence that the words sounded like a single hiss.

"I'm only curious. A would-be writer and thinker must be curious, don't you agree?"

"Not about this. It's disgusting. He's disgusting." She flicked her head toward Hoss, who was heading toward the establishment entrance.

"I don't want to endure any more of him or his world."

"I want to go in, Malany. I'm curious, and stop acting like such a snob. That's a privilege reserved for the non-poet class."

Malany loosened her grip, and Beckman pulled his arm away and stepped out of the car. Malany quickly leaned over and locked his door. She rolled the window up halfway, then, leaning into the opening, said, "Don't be alarmed if I'm not here when you and 'Igor' return from shopping."

"Tolerance, Malany. Tol—"

The window glass severed the word and the space between them, sealing Malany off in the private atmosphere of her Oldsmobile.

Beckman followed Hoss into the "Army Navy" surplus store, hesitating briefly at the turnstile, which caught him at the level of his genitals. Beckman pushed against the bar with his hip, expecting to feel an electric shock. It flipped over with a hard machine clank, the other bar rotating behind him, banging against his other hip and pushing him into the retail area.

Hoss was busy going through a stack of blue jeans, withdrawing the occasional pair and earnestly holding them up to his waist. Beckman wandered around, noticing that most of the clothing items were new and not generally of military quality. The only genuinely military clothes seemed to be in a pile of used and faded army fatigues.

Several black teenagers with tasseled wool hats were looking through the boots. A short, nervous white man with a Prince Valiant haircut, wearing a shirt printed with sunbursts, stood behind the checkout counter.

The counter was a large glass case containing what appeared to be an almost infinite variety of knives, the most prominent having blades of wavy chrome steel with imitation pearl handles. Others had blades curved or twisted in some ghastly manner. Next to that were rows of plastic Nazi helmets, plastic hand grenades and what appeared to be replica military rifles of World War I and World War II design.

"He'p you with something, buddy?" the man behind the counter asked.

"No thanks. I'm waiting for my friend."

The man looked past Beckman like a secret service agent scanning the crowd for a potential assassin. The two black teenagers came bouncing up to the counter, laughing too loudly at some private fun. They dropped a pair of boots on the counter.

The man flinched. He avoided looking at them, but looked for a long time at the price tag. Beckman saw the man's hand shaking while holding the price tag.

"Just two days ago, I was robbed," the man said after the black teenagers had left. He was suddenly friendly.

"I've only been working here a month. The fella before me was robbed twice. Everyone that comes in here is starting to give me the willies."

He looked at the door. It was slowly closing behind the two black men.

"I guess it's just beginning to get to me, huh? Looking at a gun pointed at you, and you don't know if the guy's gonna use it or not. It makes you see things really different, and it seems so unfair—I mean, him having a gun and deciding whether or not you're gonna live or die. Well, I'm ready next time."

The man's voice became stronger. Then, with the speed of a magician's coin trick, he held up a .45 caliber, M1911 pistol with faded bluing. The thing looked too heavy and massive for the man's hand and seemed, after its sudden display, to overcome the man's own strength as he slowly lowered it back below the counter.

"I keep it on me all the time I'm away from here. I've been practicing too." He pointed vigorously to the counter. "I can bring it out and fire it in less than two seconds flat."

"Have you ever really fired it?" Beckman asked.

The man's brow wrinkled. "No, not really. But don't really have to until it becomes necessary, do I? Or it's just a waste of money, ain't it? Damn bullets cost nearly 75 cents apiece. But believe me, I don't have the slightest bit of hesitancy about using it. Man's got to defend hisself. It's his right, ain't it? One thing for sure, the police can't do it."

The man seemed to relax but continued to watch Hoss. He stuffed the gun into his pants pocket, and Beckman imaginatively saw the man tugging desperately at the gun, which had caught on the edge of his pocket. That was always his problem as a kid playing cowboys and Indians, before the Christmas when he finally got the real leather police-type holster with the disappointing safety strap to hold the gun in. He had spent hours practicing his draw against the boy across the street, but the safety strap always seemed to interfere.

It was his first real decision as a budding adult. The summer before the irreversible changes began to occur: hair began to grow on his body, his taste in food changed, girls excited him in strange ways. Cutting the strap off his real police holster meant not so much a denial, but a conscious decision against adult practicality, adult authority. Almost desperately, he chose childhood one last time before biology pulled him away forever.

Beckman wanted to ask the cashier if he was afraid he might fumble, get the trigger caught in his pants—then the boy across the street says, "Bang, you're dead." And it will be the truth. But he didn't ask. The man had made his decision about adulthood. Why should he interfere?

Beckman still wanted to know, however, and he regretted again not having a fixed address so that the man could write and tell him what it was like to face another man in a real decision of life and death. There would be no falling dead act to reward the faster draw, no getting up again and demanding a rematch.

Hoss had piled up two pair of jeans, an army fatigue jacket, two khaki shirts and a fishing hat with Budweiser labels covering it. The man busied himself ringing up each item, carefully double checking before he hit the keys. Hoss paid for the items, thanked the man, and started for the car wearing his new Budweiser hat. Beckman walked past the man. He felt the shock of an outer sphere of decay and doom enveloping him. Beckman said to the man that he hoped he would never have to use the gun. The man agreed but added, slapping his bulging pocket, that he was ready just in case.

Malany had moved to the passenger's seat, a clear indication that Beckman was to drive.

"How can she stand it all closed up like that?" Hoss asked. "And listen," he continued as Beckman reached for the driver's door handle. "Why don't I drive? I can get us out of this town and down the road to Memphis in no time."

"The limit's fifty-five, Hoss."

"Oh, shit, I know that. Who don't, and who cares? The cops in this state don't enforce it."

Malany looked horrified at the prospect of Hoss driving.

"Not!" was the only word Beckman heard of her protest.

"Hey, whose car is this anyway?" Hoss asked.

"Malany's," Beckman said.

"Oh, well, I guess that makes her the Hoss then."

"Not exactly. Give her time, Hoss. She's really all right and maybe even a little special."

Hoss grinned, apparently misinterpreting the comment.

"Hoss, can't you see she's different and she wants, even likes it that way?"

"Well," Hoss continued grinning this time, pulling his Budweiser hat down over his eyes. "If you say so, buddy." They were on their way again, Hoss changing into his new clothes, indifferent to the stares from passing cars. Malany, in a sudden flurry of thought, began writing without pause in her notebook. Beckman knew that they were on their way, really on their way now, emotionally committed. They were almost one-third of the way across the country, racing like a migrating bird toward warm climes where milk and honey flowed in abundance, rolling on hot tires, thumping like tight balloons on sections of the highway leading into Memphis.

Beckman dreamed of beautiful California girls clad in brief bikinis, beckoning to him from California beaches. Everywhere his dream turned there were white-topped mountains, sandy beaches, all the elements of a carefully composed billboard advertisement. Beckman allowed himself, regardless of how unreasonable, to enjoy this new vision. It was a fantastic extreme of what he felt to be most real, where self-murder was epidemic, and the sunlight often shone as yellow as a dingy light bulb. The reality was a trash can brimming with discarded humanity, but he held out hope for the beaches. Somewhere the fantasy had to touch the reality.

Some went and preferred to stay, and not only people like him or Malany or Hoss, but real people with jobs, debts, and family who needed a clean place to spawn, people with a geography and family jewels. But could any place on earth offer what he and Malany and Hoss needed?

"Malany," Beckman blurted out. "What do you need?"

Malany was thoughtful for a moment. "I don't know. I suppose I need nothing."

"I need to take a piss," Hoss said.

"This gas station do?" Beckman said, turning into a self-service operation named GAS CITY.

"Buddy, just a hole in the ground will do," Hoss said.

Beckman stopped next to one of the end pumps and started to get out. Hoss held him by the shoulder.

"Wait here, I'll get it," Hoss said, scrambling out of the car and running slightly crouched, knees together, toward the men's room.

Malany, as usual, ignored him, then surprised Beckman by saying, "Let's spend the night here. We all need a decent rest, and I have some friends here I would like to see."

"Okay, I could do with a rest. I don't know what Hoss wants to do."

"Who cares?" Malany groaned.

"Strangely enough, Malany, I do."

"Well, he's your friend then and, I suppose, once you get used to him, he is easy to ignore."

Hoss was returning, smiling, and tipped his Budweiser hat at the teenage boy who was the sole operator of the place. Hoss switched a handle on the gas pump and started pumping gas into the car. Beckman heard only parts of what he was telling the attendant. It was something that sounded like how wonderful it was "just to be able to let it all go."

The attendant nodded and agreed, vigorously repeating, "Yep, yep, know what ya mean."

Malany got out of the car and walked past Hoss to a phone booth. Hoss paid the attendant and danced back to the car.

"Tell me something, buddy. You ever got any of that?"

Beckman was stunned, not at the blatant referral to Malany's sexuality, but at the clear mental image of Malany in the sex act, salivating with lust, groaning with pleasure, arms enveloping, legs intertwined around an invisible lover and, why, Beckman wondered, couldn't he see himself there.

Beckman laughed at the thought. "No, I never have, and want to know something else?"

Hoss leaned over the back of the seat close to Beckman's ear, grinning with anticipation.

"I don't want to, either."

Hoss dropped back, laughing. "My God, ain't it awful! Just thinking about it with her gives me a sharp pain right between the thighs."

Malany was coming back from the phone. A gust of wind whipped at her clothes. She could have been mistaken for a priestess of some obscure religious cult come to deliver the world from self-service gas stations and chlorinated swimming pools.

"Did you tell him?" Malany asked, slamming the door and locking it.

Beckman half turned to Hoss. "Malany has old friends in this town whom she wants to see. What she's trying to ask is, do you want to stick around or go on your own?"

Hoss appeared to think for a minute,

"You know, I've come this far and it ain't like I got to get there on time. Know what I mean? Yeah, I'd like to meet some of Malany's friends."

Malany grimaced, a little too theatrically Beckman thought.

"They invited us for later."

"But not for dinner, you mean?" Beckman asked.

"That's right."

"Oh Christ, more fast food hamburgers if we can afford it, or will it be garbage can salad?" Beckman asked.

"Don't worry about a thing. Ole Hoss here has got plenty of the green stuff. Let's go to some place and really put on a spread. What do you say?"

"It's okay with me, but what does Malany want to do?"

"Let's go to Overton park. It's in the center of town. Show you the way," Malany said. "There are a lot of places there to eat."

"Malany, have you been here before?" Beckman asked.

"Yes, it's a long story, long forgotten. Turn onto this road, and follow it until I tell you to turn again."

# CHAPTER 12

Professor Leon Moskowski had been professor of Syrian Literature at Western State University for the past three years, and for the same period of time, an active member of the Polish-Jewish Anti-Defamation League. His wife, Honey, whom Hoss quickly dubbed "Honey Buns," was a passionate collector of antiques, ranging from eighteenth-century whiskey bottles to Louis XIV furniture.

Professor Moskowski lamented, "She is now into antique cars, specifically a rebuilt Model A sedan. She's already put ten thousand into it. My dear wife," the professor said, patting Honey's hand, "only wants to recreate the past. Don't you, my child?"

Honey smiled. "Only what was good and grand about the past," she said, in a voice ten years younger than she was. "I think it's a worthwhile creation," she said, looking toward Malany.

"Creation costs money. Malany can attest to that," Beckman said. Malany was uncharacteristically embarrassed.

"And I still admire you for what you've done, Malany," Honey said, gazing at Malany with her most sincere expression. She went on. "Deciding once and for all that you wanted to write poetry, and going out and doing it, wonderful. Have you had much published?"

Malany glowed as one unexpectedly gifted with the stigmata, and modestly acknowledged that some of her work had appeared in commercial publications and some in university publications. Honey flashed her "how nice" smile and the professor looked interested.

"Malany," Honey continued. "If you would like to stay over for a few days . . ." Honey waited for the effect of this to settle in. "You could go with us to Dr. Pointer's poetry reading. He has this most marvelous little cabaret, decorated with paintings by local artists and, as I mentioned, every Saturday night, poetry readings. Oh, I don't know why I didn't think of it before." She smiled, bearing meat-stained teeth and red gums. "I could introduce you, and probably Pierre would like to have you read sometime."

The professor nodded in agreement. "Yes, the well of local talent is quickly running dry. They need a little invigorating mongrel blood." He laughed uproariously, spilling ash and sparks from his pipe.

"Could we hear a sample of your work?" Honey asked.

Malany opened the ever-present copy of her book and began to read from the selections that she had used for her last public reading. The professor and Honey listened with genuine interest as Malany beat out her feelings about the complexities of love and living, and finished within a tasteful half hour. The professor applauded. Honey went straight to the phone and started dialing.

"Malany," the professor said, "Your work shows definite promise."

From the phone, the voice of Honey began to dominate. "Pierre, I think you would be very impressed, she's really good. Yes, as good as that. Oh, be a dove . . . I suppose I can endure it. See you then."

Honey's long, feminine fingers replaced the phone gently. She self-consciously walked, with hard steps, back to the group and took her former seat on the carpet next to her husband's chair.

"Malany, you have to stay, at least until tomorrow night. Pierre wants to meet you, so he's invited us to a private party at the home of the head of the English department, tomorrow night. And oh," she glanced at Beckman and Hoss, "your friends are certainly welcome to come."

Hoss pretended to look at a non-existent watch. "Well, it's getting pretty late, and I hate to leave you folks, but ole Hoss has had a rough day. What do you say, good buddy?" Hoss glanced at Beckman.

"Yes, we had better be finding some place to stay," Beckman added.

"You don't have to rush off, gentlemen. You're more than welcome to spend the night here," the professor said.

Hoss stood up, followed by Beckman.

"Thank you just the same, but me and Beckman here would just be in the way." Hoss quickly started for the door. Beckman and the professor followed. Beckman turned to Malany.

"Can we borrow your car tonight?"

Malany nodded her consent, reluctantly. Beckman hated to take advantage, but events seemed to be working against him.

"Don't worry, I'll take care of it." He hoped she would believe him and realize also that he would not let Hoss drive the car.

"Will you be coming to the party?" Honey injected.

"Maybe," Hoss said.

"Well, if you decide to go, we'll leave here at eight, okay?"

The professor was shaking Hoss's hand, and he patted Beckman on the shoulder as they passed by him.

"Why don't you fellas come along tomorrow night? I promise you it will not be as stuffy as Honey makes it sound."

Hoss was already out of the door and walking fast toward the car.

Beckman had the feeling that Hoss was actually running and that if he didn't get through the door, Hoss would leave without hesitating. Beckman hurriedly brushed by the professor and said something to the effect that he and Hoss would probably see them tomorrow night.

Beckman remained quiet until he heard the front door of the house close. Hoss was waiting by the car.

"Hey, Hoss. Wait!" Hoss got into Malany's Oldsmobile and Beckman followed, stopping just long enough to remove Malany's bags from the trunk.

"Why did you leave like that? I thought they were very nice, considering two perfect strangers come into their home and wait for an invitation of free room and board."

"Didn't you see it, buddy?"

"See what?"

"That professor. I couldn't take it anymore, him staring at my cock like that. I thought he was going to start drooling all over his goddamn gray beard."

"That's crazy, Hoss."

"How would you know, buddy? The way you were watching Honey Buns bounce her things around. 'Course, I don't blame you. She's something to watch, and I imagine she's one good piece. It don't make sense, her being friends with Malany."

"Hoss, the professor has very thick glasses. Maybe it only appeared . . ."

"Ah shit, boy. I been around long enough to know a fag when I see one. Now do us a favor, buddy, and let's get out of here."

Beckman started the car and drove away. "Well, suppose you're right, so what? What difference should that make?"

"Listen, good buddy. I don't care what anybody does. He can suck an army of dicks as far as I care, as long as mine ain't one of them."

"I still say you might have imagined it."

"Okay, supposin' I did, I wasn't going to stick around and find out."

"What did you expect him to do, rape you right there in front of his wife?"

Hoss laughed. "You never know, what with gay liberation and all."

"Let's forget about it. Nothing happened. What do we do now?"

"First thing is to stop at the first liquor store we see and pick up a bottle, then find a cheap motel room and see what we can stock it with in the way of female companionship."

Hoss ran into the shopping center liquor store, bowlegged in his new western-style jeans. After a few minutes he ran back out, clutching under his arm a brown paper bag in the shape of a quart bottle, twisted at the neck. He leapt in the car and began peeling back the bag from the bottle neck. He wrung the cap off and, before Beckman had cleared the parking lot, began sucking from the bottle.

"Fella in there says Overton Square is the place for the choice meat, but there's another place over near Cleveland Street for a little rougher trade in dark stuff, and maybe a butt load of penicillin afterwards."

"Look, Hoss, I don't go in for this sort of thing—besides, I'm broke."

"Hey man, I got enough for both of us. When's the last time you had a nice piece of ass?"

"Come on, Hoss. There is no need for that."

"O-o-o-h shit, sounds like some of what's wrong with Malany has rubbed off on you."

"And what do you think's wrong with Malany?" Beckman snapped.

Hoss settled back, resembling a soft, plastic, life-size cowboy in total relaxation. "Malany is dead, boy. At least she might as well be. She don't feel nothin'."

"Hoss, you may have the wrong impression of Malany, and me. I may not fully understand her, she may be a little eccentric to you, but she does feel, and feel deeply. How on earth could anyone write poetry and not feel? And I mean good poetry. I've read her work, and I like most of it."

"Now Beckman, you're an educated man. You should already

know what it's taken me years of fucking up to learn. I mean, the only way a person lives and knows is by feeling and, my God, you have to know it in your gut first. It's got to tingle. Then, if you have time, you can know it in your head. Do you see what I'm driving at, boy?"

"Yes, but you're wrong about Malany. She may not be a people's poet, but it's because she lives on a different plane."

"By that you mean superior?" Hoss sneered.

"Yes, I guess that is what I mean. At least she is superior to me in many ways."

"Man, that ain't nothing but college jive. I tell you, just watch old Hoss tonight and learn firsthand that people are animals first, and right down to that hot core of their bodies is the soul of an animal. And boy, most people, the honest ones that is, have come to the conclusion that it ain't so bad.

"Most people—the ones I like, that is—have come to recognize this in others, and they want to share it. They want to mingle all that good animal feeling about life with each other. Them's my kind of people. Your Malany's nothing but a mess of self-love. I'll bet she wouldn't sell one of those books of hers for any amount. She's a zombie, boy, and she's going to make you into one if you don't break away.

"Besides," Hoss said after a long hesitation. "She's a phony, Beckman, only she don't know it."

"And how do you know that, Hoss."

"I can spot 'em boy. I can always spot 'em—maybe because I'm a little bit of a phony myself."

"Do you think I'm a phony, Hoss?"

Hoss looked a little stunned. His eyes moved rapidly from side to side as his brain searched for an answer.

"I think you're after something you can't get."

Beckman was tempted to enquire further but decided he did

not want to reach the conclusion of this conversation. He shifted the verbal momentum back to their earlier discussion.

"You mean you want us to just go steal the car and leave Malany there, with those people?"

"Well, they're her friends, ain't they? I mean, you saw how she was, right at home. I bet she's already shit-canned you and me both."

"I can't do it now, Hoss. A few days ago, maybe I could have, but I can't do it now."

Hoss shrugged. "Okay, boy. Do it your way, but . . . " Hoss became silent. Morose lines appeared on his face. He lifted the bottle, and Beckman watched as several air bubbles escaped up the neck. He couldn't condemn Hoss or even criticize him. Why shouldn't Hoss, in all of his tragic glory, not enjoy the luxury of simplification? The crying need for sex, the crying need to eat, to periodically induce mild delirium with cheap whiskey and reach, at times, swift clarity in his literal mind that reflected the surreal laments of Malany's poetry.

Hoss had quickly lowered the level in the bottle by a third before Beckman found his way to Overton Square and had safely parked the car. They ambled down Madison Avenue, past pastel-colored boutiques offering "giveaway" specials for the young scene. Hoss peered in windows, frightening salesgirls and drawing angry looks from male escorts. He insisted on having a drink in every bar. He approached cab drivers and was ignored or laughed at. Bejeweled black pimps treated him with indifference or suspicion.

It was his manner: too loud, too obvious. Even the occasional "working girl" ducked inside at the sight of Hoss. He was simply too unbelievable. He was what others acted like. By midnight Hoss was beginning to tire and even to show signs of discouragement.

They were in a place called Pearl's, and Hoss had decided to stay. He liked the local talent playing the progressive jazz of the fifties, and he was beginning to use the language of the sportsman to explain his lack of success. "But only for tonight. Tomorrow we hunt in a different part of the woods," he sputtered.

The liquor seemed to hit him all at once, knocking his eyes into whirling concentric wheels, relaxing the muscles in his face until its separate parts—nose, cheeks, and chin—all seemed to hang in fleshy bags. It seemed an almost complete metamorphosis, a physical representation of the irrational. Beckman was thinking of a way to extricate Hoss, or whatever Hoss had become, without an incident when two women, ensconced in the uniform of the streetwalker, came up to the table.

"They look like the ones, Crystal."

"Yeah," said Crystal.

Hoss raised his swaying head and slowly, through glazed eyes, saw that his efforts were about to pay off. "See, buddy. See?"

"You the fellas who want dates?"

"Dates? Us, honey," Hoss said.

"Let's go outside where we can talk." The prostitutes glanced nervously around.

Hoss rose, steadied himself, and led the way through the crowd of bar patrons. Beckman noticed that people made way for a drunk much quicker than for someone sober. He and the prostitutes, supporting Hoss between them, moved hurriedly to the car. No one spoke. Urgency propelled them. Beckman was reluctant, and they knew Hoss was about to collapse. They stopped at the car. The prostitutes looked it over.

"You look real enough," said the biggest one, in the blonde wig and imitation fur jacket. "But how do we know that you ain't cops? So many of 'em think they're on television these days."

"Believe me, sweetheart, we ain't cops. Would a cop be this damn drunk?" Hoss blurted out. "And just soes we can be nice to one another, do you two beauties have real names?"

The big blonde half smiled and said, "Yeah, she's Crystal and I'm Chandelier. Good enough for ya?"

"Fiiine," Hoss slurred. "Beautiful names, worthy of my friend here." He waved his hand toward Beckman.

"I seen 'em every way, honey," Chandelier said to Crystal while leaning over to check Hoss's breath. "Wh-e-e-e, honey: You've about had it. What about him?" She nodded toward Beckman.

"He's with me. He's all right, but still a virgin at heart." Hoss laughed and fell forward but was caught by the blonde and repositioned against the car.

"Okay, honey. It's a hundred for a straight fuck, a hundred and fifty more to go down, three hundred for both, and twenty percent more for extra turn-ons. Absolutely no rough stuff, no whips, knives, or blood. Okay?"

Hoss nodded and started to fall forward again. The prostitute grabbed him by the shoulders and shook him until there were groans of protest.

"Listen," she said to Beckman. "You fellas got a room?"

"No," Beckman said.

"Christ, what a night. Well, we'll have to do the best we can."

She opened the back door of the Oldsmobile, aimed Hoss through the open door, and pushed.

"Okay, honey," she said to Beckman. "Drive us. I know a quiet place that ain't so well lit."

The other prostitute, Crystal, started to get in on the passenger side.

"No," Beckman almost shouted.

"What?"

"It's not for me."

"Well, Mr. Goody-Two-shoes, it's going to cost your friend double."

"Ish aw'rite, boy. Nubble or nothin'," Hoss managed to say.

"Come on, we ain't got all night," said Chandelier. "Just drive us around. Then I'll let you know. You can even watch. You might change your mind by the time we get back." Chandelier laughed, a practiced, mirthless bar room laugh.

Beckman tried to apologize to Crystal, but she ignored it and looked, instead, with considerable irritation as her partner climbed into the back seat. Beckman drove away, leaving the young prostitute standing alone next to the empty parking space, her bare legs looking thin and vulnerable.

The blonde worked furiously trying to peel off Hoss's stiff new jeans. The western belt buckle clinked like a small bell as she worked first at the waist, then pulled and jerked them farther down the legs. She pulled and tugged and grunted and cursed until she finally cleared the last obstacle and Hoss's pants lay wadded around his knees. Next came Hoss's jockey shorts, which she rolled into something resembling a giant white rubber band.

"Oh, Jesus," she said to Beckman, "this ain't gonna work. Are you sure you wouldn't like to turn a trick, sweetie? I'll even throw in a few extras, free."

Beckman had to stop for a red light. All language seemed to evaporate from his mind. He tried moving his lips, hoping the right words would fall out, but nothing. All he could do was look in the rearview mirror where he could see Hoss, totally passed out sitting upright, his head lolling on the back of the seat like a loose ball. Chandelier was frantically struggling to open the door, her hands full of Hoss's money. She popped it open. The noise sounded like a gunshot. She was running. Beckman hit the accelerator, skidding the car around, and followed, relieved that the traffic light had turned green at the same moment.

Chandelier, unencumbered by her dress, which flogged in the

wind around her hips, ran with amazing speed. Beckman passed her, saw her image momentarily frozen in the strobe effect of his passing headlights. She was a grotesque wingless bird, running with great white legs and featherless wings, pumping the air in a useless, forgotten attempt at flight.

He swung the car to the curb, skidded, and screamed to a stop. He leapt out and saw her turn and run in the opposite direction. He caught up with her quickly, but as he reached for the flying skirt she turned and darted like a gazelle to the left, now between two buildings in a space too small for vehicles but wide enough for a single person to run through. She was a natural, that prostitute, an undiscovered track star, and she ran as though she was truly running for her life.

Beckman thought that he was going to lose her. She was gaining distance. She reached the end of the space and made a quick turn to the right, behind the building. Beckman was sure that he had lost her then, but he heard the unmistakable clashing of metal trashcans and the dull thudding of soft material falling on the pavement. Beckman rounded the corner of the building and saw the prostitute struggling, like a netted tiger, amid a falling pyramid of cardboard boxes and trashcans. He knew that this would be his last chance to retrieve Hoss's money. Having a sudden, strong desire not to spend the night in the car with Hoss, Beckman sprinted with his last reserve of strength toward the fallen prostitute. Seeing Beckman lunging toward her and assuming the worst, she held up her hands in surrender.

"Don't hit me. Don't hit my face, for God's sake."

But Beckman, already airborne in a final lunge toward his target, could not, regardless of how hard he wished it, change the irrevocable force of impact. Together they tumbled deeper into the pile of boxes, and for a while there was silence from their cubistic pyramid. Beckman pushed aside the boxes and crawled out of his entombment, dragging the prostitute by the hand and apologizing like a dazed victim of a tragedy.

The prostitute stopped pleading and fell to her knees in a posture of one about to be executed. Beckman pulled back her fingers from the wadded money and carefully extracted the bills from her hands. He flattened each bill out, neatly folded them, and put them into his pocket.

"I'm not going to hurt you," Beckman assured her. He turned to walk away.

"Are you sure you wouldn't like just one trick, mister? I can make you feel things you've never felt before."

Beckman didn't answer or look back. One hesitation, one moment of pity, and he would not be able to walk away with the money. She continued to plead, even as Beckman blindly stumbled down the hideous gap between the buildings. He covered his ears with his hands so that his own racing blood would drown out her cries, and he did not uncover them until he was back in the car with all the windows closed and the doors locked.

# CHAPTER 13

It was after three a.m. before Beckman found a cheap motel still open. He unloaded himself and Hoss into its cheerless interior. There were two beds, both sagging in the middle, but nothing mattered now but sleep. He dumped Hoss onto one of them, making sure that he was lying on his side. He could breathe easier this way and if he threw up, he would not choke on his own vomit. Beckman then took a shower, staying under the hot water for a long time to release the twisted cords of his nerves and muscles. The motel's towel had a large hole in the center, and it was small, half the size of a regular towel, but he made do.

He felt exhausted and fell into bed with the expectation of instant sweet sleep. Sleep did not come, however; at least not for a long time, not until the light of the coming day began to make gray-black shadows on the wall opposite the window. Only then did something switch off in Beckman's mind, and he stopped seeing the prostitutes who had made the night their home.

Beckman thought about them all and about what he felt for them, especially why he had felt no anger toward the prostitute who had stolen Hoss's money. Most bothersome, however, was an expanding wedge of fear that none of them were ever going to reach California.

Hoss was still drunk late that afternoon when Beckman roused him out of an alcoholic sleep and pushed him under the trickle of water passing for a shower. He was drunk on the way to Overton Park where Beckman stopped to kill a few hours so that Hoss could sober up before going to the professor's home.

They walked through the park, stopped by the pond to watch the ducks, and browsed through the small art gallery so that Hoss could see the nudes.

"All fat," was Hoss's observation. "Why did them artists all like fat women?"

"I don't know, Hoss, maybe fat women were considered beautiful, looked upon as healthy and sensuous."

Hoss made a face of disapproval. They walked around for a while longer, Hoss perking up and noticing the girls. They stopped at a McDonald's before going on to the professor's. Hoss ate two quarter pounders, claiming that meat and bread were the only things that could sober him up.

The professor greeted Hoss and Beckman warmly. The atmosphere was jolly in the home. Honey dashed around doing last minute household things. They were offered brandy and cigars, which they refused. Even Hoss turned a bit pale at the suggestion. Malany had even dressed in a light blue suit, borrowed from Honey, which looked unexpectedly natural on her. With her hair pulled back, she looked strangely like a mature, young English professor. She was seated on the sofa, her book and a black notebook tucked securely under her arm. She waited patiently for Honey, who finally burst from her room bedecked in a long, white evening gown and jewels. The appearance seemed timed to dazzle. It did bring Hoss to the edge of his seat and, for a moment, stunned Beckman with the realization that he was in the presence of a truly beautiful woman.

"Malany, please don't be offended, but I think it's best if we go in our cars. I mean, your car is so old and can't possibly be in the best repair."

Malany looked as though the thought had never occurred to her that her car was old, in need of repair, and that her friend feared it as she would fear an ailing and unpredictable animal. It wasn't because of this new awareness that she consented, it was the usual disregard for the trivial. Deciding on a means of transportation seemed vastly unimportant. It was a concern of people who always worry about what they will eat or what they will wear. Malany's face looked as elongated and as expressionless as ever.

"Good," Honey said, "you and your friend can go with Leon and, Beckman, you go with me in the Model A."

Leon smiled and nodded his approval.

The arrangements seemed at once suspicious to Beckman, and he knew, from the way Hoss looked at him, that Hoss felt betrayed and defenseless. Beckman, stunned, groped at nearly the speed of light for an adequate protest and only vaguely considered Honey's rationale that a Model A could be safer and newer than a 1970 Oldsmobile. Beckman found himself tagging along with the others, all following like a school of fish behind Honey.

Outside, Hoss, in a tone of desperation, expressed the desire to see Honey's Model A. Before Honey could respond, Hoss was standing beside the car and pretending to inspect it in the dim light of the garage.

Honey was talking with Malany in the professor's car. "Buddy," Hoss whispered, "I don't like what's going on. Now I'm only going along with this because I want us all to go to California. You know, it's become a kind of thing with me. But I can't take much more of these creeps. So, buddy, you do what you have to, then let's get out of here."

"What about Malany?" Beckman asked.

"Well, you can handle her. I can't." Hoss slapped the hood of the Model A and said, loud enough for all to hear, "Yeah, they sure don't build 'em like this anymore."

He waved tauntingly to Honey, who was now sitting behind the steering wheel of her Model A, and walked back across the front yard to the professor's car. Beckman felt a strong surge of admiration for Hoss; the inexplicable rightness of his vanity, his uncluttered knowing of the present, all somehow geared to his wonderful ability to take action.

Beckman felt swept away and thrust in the middle of a torrential stream. He almost blurted out that he didn't care about riding in a Model A. He hated the false past of antiques and Model A's as much as he fumed with passion at the sight of her.

But the feelings subsided, and he found himself riding in the soft, rolled leather seat of the Model A. The engine ticking along like a toy car and Honey, with her silken blonde hair, her flashing jewels, her non-stop femme chatter and the indefinable darkness outside, did seem to transport him to 1928. It was as though the ideas and feeling of the time had been forged with the car's carbon, oxygen, and iron, into the real substance and form of the car. Beckman began to think seriously about Prohibition, the dying gasp of Puritanism, the loss of faith in capitalism, the frenzied, unabashed assault on the vestiges of the nineteenth century. He felt it all as deeply as if he were there.

It seemed such sensible madness as he stepped out of the car onto the grounds of a solid home, rooted firmly among ancient trees and dated, unquestionably, before the Civil War. Pierre greeted them at the door, an individual smile and handshake for everyone but in the general don't-give-a-damn manner of his French ancestors.

"Oh," he said, clasping his hands a bit too theatrically. "So, you are our young poetess. We are anxious to hear you. Honey has said so much about you and your work."

He took Malany's hand in both of his as if he had been wearing a Cardinal's habit. Beckman thought he could have been the essence of a Renaissance prince of the church seeking favors.

"I want you to meet our young poet in residence, John Darling." Pierre snickered. "Oh, don't laugh, dear. It's really his name."

He led Malany by her still captive hand across the room

to a large man with Walt Whitman hair and beard, but dressed conventionally in a clean tie and jacket. The poet stood off, just away from the main body of people who had gathered in the library where the reading was to take place. He talked quietly with several students and occasionally cast a contemptuous glance around the room. He was already acquainted with the professor and his wife and thrust his hand toward Malany. He said, in a tone suggesting esteem, that he was looking forward to hearing her work. Beckman was introduced and dispensed with. Then Hoss, who momentarily silenced the room by mispronouncing the poet's name, said:

"What was that again? John Dillinger, you said?"

"Darling. John Darling," the poet whispered.

"Darling, John Darling," Hoss repeated with contrasting volume. "Well, I just think that's just a darling name."

Hoss laughed. The poet was clearly taken aback. His bespectacled eyes went into uncontrolled fluttering and, it seemed to Beckman, that his face and body visibly deflated.

A bell tinkled, announcing the start of the reading, and all present moved in loose groups to prearranged rows of chairs. Some, mostly students, found places on the carpet, where they casually leaned against shelves of rare books. One girl, dressed in house painter's coveralls and a train engineer's cap, leaned casually against an early English translation of Homer.

The poet lurched toward the wooden stand where he placed his notebook. Looking more formidable against the background of a wall of books, he began, to Beckman's disappointment, by clearing his throat and reading one of his recent works, "Where is Love?"

Beckman looked around at all of the pretty, intelligent, gifted people, listening intently to Darling's rhythmic recitations of "my hard cock," "your sweet cunt, kissed before and behind," "young breasts that bring forth the milk of life, where is love?" Honey seemed mesmerized. Malany stared straight ahead like a priestess and Hoss, slouching in his metal chair, tried to talk with the woman next to him.

Darling finished the poem and acknowledged the excited applause which followed. Then he launched into what he said was the rewriting of *Paradise Lost*, showing Satan as a liberator of, and the misunderstood symbol of, Puritan sexual repression. After thirty minutes of this, a fog of boredom had settled in the room, stunning everyone with a paralysis that maintained the appearance of attention, but severed their awareness at the optical nerve.

Darling had finished a full minute before a general applause rippled through the audience, and the stillness was broken by sporadic hand clapping. The poet smiled broadly and waved like the Pope from the balcony of the Papal residence. Beckman suspected that Darling had misinterpreted the audience's reaction.

Malany was next. She walked up to the stand, deliberately slowing her movements. She placed her opened book on the stand and, for a few long moments, gazed around at the people in the room until it was as quiet as a laboratory sound chamber. Then she read her best works as they should be read, stressing and hesitating at the right places for the best aesthetic effect. Beckman realized, hearing her read this way and making a blood-sweating effort to do her best, that he had only read her poems with his eyes.

He was seized with shame and guilt and, in the accompanying sense of helplessness, forgot about Honey, who had begun, sometime during the reading, to press her leg against his. Beckman, at that moment, realized the unbridgeable gap between them, and knew also that if somehow the great mystery of things had been different, he and Malany could have loved, and there could have been love to fill the distance. They could have been writers together, or school teachers, anything. And, for the first time since Herschel had urinated on him, tears burned his eyes.

"Oh, Malany." The words bubbled from his throat in a hoarse sigh. "What?" Honey whispered next to his ear. "What did you say?"

Beckman didn't answer. He could not. Not until Malany had finished and Darling had leapt to his feet, leading the audience, clapping and yelling, "Bravo! Bravo! Bravo!"

The rest of the room, following his example, rose and applauded. Some rushed to talk to Malany before she left her place by the stand. Malany had, at last, tasted success and recognition, however small, from a literary establishment.

As the excitement subsided, people began drifting into the next several rooms, all wretchedly decorated in French Rococo. Beckman thought he could hear the music of Couperin coming from the walls, almost totally masked by the general noise of people and tinkling glasses. Honey led him to the punch bowl where she ordered drinks for both, and a delicate French cheese on a tasteless wafer. Hoss had followed them and ordered a glass topped with bourbon and as many wafers of cheese as he could hold in one hand.

"Listen, buddy," he said the moment Honey's attention was taken by a talkative guest. "This fella Moskowski is really hot. The son of a bitch won't leave me alone."

"Well, why don't you just tell him no, Hoss?"

"I would, but he ain't asked me yet, and if I make the wrong move before then and piss him off, it could mean trouble for you and Malany, and I don't want to do that. Especially now."

Beckman looked over at Malany, who had now transformed into a flushed, talking creature basking joyfully in her microfame.

"You see, boy," Hoss said in a whisper, "I'm afraid Malany's done forgot all about California and all about you and me." Hoss stopped abruptly as Honey quickly broke off her conversation and returned.

"Malany has made quite a hit, and it seems that Darling is very enthused," Honey said. "Poor boy, he gets all juiced up over anything new. He goes nearly crazy each year when the new crop of coeds pour in. And Malany, being a struggling poetess, desperate, vulnerable, and all that, has probably excited him to near madness."

The professor came up beside Hoss and was greeted with an icy stare from his wife. Beckman felt the flash of a wordless, but clearly understood communication between them.

"Come, Beckman. I want you to meet a few people." Honey grabbed him by the hand and towed him across the room to a straight-backed man in his fifties with wavy gray hair, all of which seemed to be tumbling over his forehead.

"Malany tells me that you're interested in ESP. I thought you would like to meet Dr. Drew of the Psychology department. He's done a lot of work in that sort of thing."

Beckman went through the formality of introduction, handshakes, smiles, little jokes, until he felt reckless and challenging. He asked the doctor how he felt about psychokinesis.

"Nothing, young man," the doctor said. Beckman took it, and correctly, as a put-down. "I am a scientist. I don't make judgements on the basis of feeling. But I will tell you what the research has shown, and that is that there is no basis for the claims of parapsychology. Oh, I know what people have said, what they have claimed. But, subjected to controlled experimentation, they simply don't hold up. There are no constants, no predictability, nothing really to give these claims appreciable validity." Dr. Drew tossed out these words as though he were brushing away annoying flies.

"Well, perhaps your experimental situations were all wrong to begin with?" Beckman said and, as he persisted, Dr. Drew's face tightened into death mask rigidity. "I mean, maybe it's close to, if not dependent on, a more primitive survival mechanism. Take, for example, people who have been victims of armed robberies. They see the gun, their minds go into slow motion, something happens, and the robber misses with every shot. What I'm saying is, maybe the intense energy of self-preservation, combined with the superior human mind, may generate a kind of energy that has limited control over material objects. It would seem to me that it might even indicate a new avenue of human evolution"

Dr. Drew shrugged. "Are you suggesting that I go out and point a gun at somebody, pull the trigger, and see what happens?"

"No, but I think it's worthwhile paying a little more attention to those who have had the experience."

"Simple-minded trash for tabloids," Dr. Drew almost shouted. He whirled around to face Honey. "I'd be more careful next time, if I were you," he said, spitting the words out so that Beckman saw drops of saliva arching all around Honey's face. Dr. Drew strode hurriedly away, back straight, head erect.

"What did he mean by that?" Beckman asked.

"Oh, nothing. Really, dear. You shouldn't have needled him like that. He has a heart condition, and I understand from his wife that he's been impotent for years." She slipped her arm through Beckman's, impulsively. "Let's get out of here. I've had enough of these people." And she meant it.

"What about them?" Beckman said, looking back to find Hoss and Malany.

"Oh, they'll come back with Leon or something. I get the impression that your friend Hoss can take care of himself, and I know Malany can. Come on, Beckman, I want to go for a ride in the Model A."

Hoss waved him on and shouted across the room, hands cupped over his mouth, "See you back at the ranch, boy."

"Really, Beckman. All of this row about the genuineness of the common man, his innate nobility, his honesty and alienation simply isn't fashionable any more. You know, you should tell your friend Hoss that the 'good ole boy' mystique is no longer charming. "

"You think he's a phony, huh?" Beckman asked.

"No, he's genuine enough. But I do think he enjoys himself

a little too much, at the expense of others," Honey said, slowly dragging Beckman toward the door.

"From what I've seen, you should know." Beckman felt the left corner of his mouth curling up into a kind of snarl like a dog sniffing at a stranger.

"Now, Beckman, there's no point in being insolent. I want us to have a pleasant ride in the country in my beautiful Model A. It can be 1928 again. You can be F. Scott Fitzgerald, or anyone you would like to be, dear, so long as it's consistent with the period."

"Mrs. Moskowski, I'm satisfied being Beckman. I don't see that I have to choose."

"Oh, but you do, dearest. You can be anybody you want to be. Let's go. I'll be a young Dorothy Parker. That should be interesting, and you can be a young Ernest Hemingway, with everyone raving about your latest book. We can go dashing about the countryside with the whole world at our fingertips. You know how to speak like Hemingway don't you—you know those pithy sentences that hit you like a bullet, the poignant word that had so much implied meaning in it. It would be very fulfilling, maybe even a little erotic, if you would give it a try."

"Good Lord, Mrs. Moskowski, that's sick. It's crazy."

"Yes, but that's what makes it so much fun. You're free to play, and believe, like a child. It's like when you discovered that sex wasn't a sin anymore. It's a whole new world now. Don't you see?"

Beckman wanted to protest against the way Honey was tugging on his arm, dragging him forcibly out of the house, whispering "come on" like the hissing of a cat. He could have stopped it right there. He could have said "no" and let it go at that, but he was curious, and he felt some responsibility for Malany. He didn't want to be the instrument of destruction, this time, by angering her friend who was beginning to seem somehow superhuman.

Honey headed south on Interstate 55. Cars passed them, sounding more like jet airplanes, some angrily sounding their horns. She ignored them and continued chatting about *A Farewell to Arms*.

"Tell me, Ernest, did you consciously intend to make Catherine so shallow? Is she your idea of what a woman should be, fatuous and completely devoted?"

"Come on, Mrs. Moskowski, this is nuts." Beckman shouted into the din of traffic noises, but he realized that she was not hearing him. Some transformation had taken place. It wasn't really a case of multiple personality. Beckman sensed that she was aware of who she really was. She was more like a neurotic actress, pretending almost to the point of insanity, but remaining sane.

"You know, Ernest, people are not saying good things about you, leaving that sweet Hadley and latching on to Pauline's money. Selfish and unnecessarily cruel, that's what I hear."

"My God, Mrs. Moskowski, this has gone far enough. It's . . ."

Honey veered sharply onto a right-hand exit and another right turn at the intersection onto an unlighted hard-surfaced road.

"This is Mississippi, Ernest. I just love driving through Mississippi. Oh, and you know, your colleague William Faulkner lives not far from here. I would suggest stopping by, but I know you two aren't on the best of terms."

Honey was clearly insisting on her fantasy. Beckman felt that, even though she wasn't truly insane or drunk, the only thing for him to do was to play along. He knew it was leading somewhere, perhaps even following (as it seemed) some circuitous plan. The design began to show when she made another turn down a dirt road. Beckman asked her if she had seen Faulkner lately.

"Just last week. He loves to go riding like this."

Beckman wondered who had played that role. Then another right turn down a much narrower dirt road. They rode for about a mile when Honey stopped the car and switched off the engine. Beckman, still curious, waited for the next event, which came rather quickly when Honey threw her arms around his neck.

"Oh Ernest, let's make love."

Whatever it was—the perfume, Honey's luscious body, the thrill of adultery—whatever it was, the desire for Honey's body swept over him so swiftly and powerfully that he was unable to move.

She unfastened his pants deftly and, with a simple, single, downward motion, jerked them down around his ankles. Then, with acrobatic expertise, she started undressing herself as she fondled Beckman's swelling genitals. Then she rose and clamored into the back seat. He saw her beautiful legs scissoring the air as she kicked to get over. Beckman followed but caught his pants on something, and in a frantic effort to free himself, heard something rip. The releasing force sent him lunging against the back of the rear seat. Honey lay writhing and moaning, her lovely legs and bottom spread grotesquely across the back seat.

"Hurry, hurry."

Beckman, slightly dizzy from the heat of the moment, felt himself plunging in with slick and surprising ease. He surrendered himself, in only a few moments, to nature's sweetest and greatest demand, all the while remaining oddly aware of his peculiar surroundings, of the mosquitoes biting his bottom and of the abnormally loud squeak of the car's springs.

"Oh, I dearly love screwing in the backseat of a Model A in the woods of Mississippi. It's so regenerative, so wonderfully primitive. How do you feel, Ernest? Can you do it again? That was so fast."

She ran her hand down to Beckman's genitals.

"Oh, you're limp. Well, we'll just have to do something about that."

"Really, Mrs. Moskowski, don't you think we had better be going?" Beckman said.

She mumbled something unintelligible, and after a few minutes of her special technique, words and considerations were again made insignificant. Somewhere in this timeless world of agony and desire, she stopped and backed up to him.

"Do it this way, and touch my boobs. Oh God, yes!"

There was a third time after a sufficient rest period; Honey on top and humping tirelessly for what seemed to Beckman like hours. At last she groaned and fell limp over Beckman's body. Beckman, in spite of his strong wish to get dressed, fell irresistibly asleep.

# CHAPTER 14

It was the sun finding a slit in the trees and through the back window of the Model A that woke them. That, and the muzzle of a twelve-gauge shotgun leveled at the top of Beckman's head. Beckman looked down the barrel in horror, at the face of a wrinkled, whiskered old man peering back at him along the barrel with one good eye, the other white and dead as a stone.

"Jonny, look at this, would you?"

Beckman looked over at the face of a mongrel dog leaning, paws up, on the front seat.

"Jonny, what do you suppose they been up to?"

Honey now realized their situation and screamed. Instantly the man cocked the hammer on the gun.

"Wait!" Beckman yelled, "Wait! Take it easy. We're not after anything. We got lost, and we're engaged to be married." Beckman could not keep the tremor out of his voice.

"That so, huh?" The man looked skeptical. "Well, suppose you all get your clothes on and don't try anythin', you hear?"

"Right, right," Beckman said, juggling to get his pants on and not caring about the rip in the crotch. Honey, visibly trembling and making an unconscious whining sound, reached frantically for her clothes.

"Listen, mister, what's the reason for holding a gun on us? We haven't done anything to you."

"Did you hear that, Jonny?"

The dog barked and lowered his ears.

"They say they ain't done nothin'. Hit's my guess is one of 'em's married and they been out here all night doing somethin' they ought not ta, and they just happen to be doing it on my place. And, Jonny, how do we know they ain't the law? The law does some mighty strange things these days."

"Your place?" Beckman said, looking around.

"Right over there."

The man pointed with his free hand while still holding the gun on them with the other. Beckman began to make out a small structure, almost completely covered by trees, with a single path leading up to it. Rusted and burned out bodies of cars representing three decades lay scattered all around the structure.

"Now," the man said, backing away, the gun still leveled at Beckman's head. "You two get out real slow and let's all go up to my place. And remember, any notions and you don't have to worry about the sins of this world anymore."

"Look, mister," Honey said, "just let us go. We didn't mean anything. I'll pay you any amount you ask. I have money, please!"

"I bet you would, you Jezebel. And is it you who's out being unfaithful to your husband? My God, if you don't look like a married woman to me. Now, no more talking. Go along."

Beckman took Honey by the hand. It was cold and trembling. He felt its bony frame under the flesh, not at all the warm, soft thing that had caressed him so tenderly during the night.

They walked quickly together, ahead of the man, always aware of the gun at their backs. They walked past the burned-out hulks, up the path to the man's cavernous dwelling. Somewhere behind the place, a chorus of howls rose.

"Just my bird dogs. Have to keep 'em locked up or they'd be all over the place. Old Jonny here's my watch dog. He ain't much for pedigree, but he's got more brains than all them pure bloodhounds put together."

The walk had taken much longer than Beckman had estimated.

He and Honey were panting as much from exhaustion as from fear. They stopped at the door.

"Can we rest a minute?" Beckman asked, entertaining somewhere in his mind the theatrical possibility of escape and rejecting simultaneously any hope of reasoning with the old man. The man, himself, had obviously rejected or had never even considered a reasonable life. Great pictures of the craziness of Beckman's life flashed on and off in his mind. Isolation and murder could never have been a part of it. He would have drawn the line there. He was sure of that.

"Inside," the man commanded, waving the barrel toward the door.

Honey looked at Beckman with such sick terror that he almost surrendered to the impulse to throw himself bodily on the man, but the old man goaded him with the barrel of the gun and they stumbled into the dark, windowless interior of the man's home.

"Over in the corner."

Slowly, still clutching each other's hand, Beckman and Honey made their way into the shack by the light of a kerosene lamp, and past the central wood table littered with the remains of a half-eaten fowl.

Honey crouched in a corner, holding her legs next to her body. Beckman squatted beside her, not taking his eyes off the shotgun which was now leveled at them from the man's seat at the table.

"What are you going to do with us?" Honey shrieked.

The man shrugged. "Don't know. I ain't had nothing to eat in the past two days but this old wild duck, and he's pretty near gone to the bad. Wild game just don't keep very long. Hell, if I get hungry enough, I just might eat one of you. Or," the man laughed, "both of you. Save going out huntin' and using up shells."

Honey started crying and Beckman, stunned by the horrifying image of being chopped up like a cut of beef, was even more revolted at the thought of his body turning to feces inside the bowels of this madman. The man brought a half gallon ceramic jug out from under the table and, without taking his eye from his captives, drained the remaining contents. He slammed the empty jug on the table.

"I hope you folks got some money."

Honey shouted, "Yes, yes! I have!"

"How much?"

"As much as you want. You can have it all."

The man smiled, baring his yellow gums, and said that he only needed enough for another jug. That was all the money he required from the world.

"What about other things? Don't you need money for those? Your guns and fuel—things like that?"

"Hell, ma'am, I suppose I do but you see, I just don't worry about them till the time comes. Right now, all I need is another jug. Everything else will take care of itself."

"I can get you one, the best whiskey money can buy," Honey said.

Beckman looked at her with surprise.

"Yes, yes." She shook her head wildly. "I have a whole quart, hasn't been opened."

"Where?" the man asked.

"Let me take you to it. I keep it hidden."

Tears were running down Honey's cheeks, but her voice was surprisingly controlled. The man sighted down the barrel and cocked the hammer. He was not to be played with.

"For Christ's sake, tell him!" Beckman shouted.

"In the car. Under the front seat."

"Now that's some hiding place," the man said, lowering the gun. "You know, Jonny, I believe that the little lady here was planning to make a run for it and leave her boyfriend behind. You see what I tell you, Jonny, about women, just can't trust 'em a-tall. I guess I'll have to fix it so's they'll stay put."

He stood up, walked a few paces over to the wall, and lifted a small coil of line from a peg.

"Now get on your bellies and hands behind you."

Beckman and Honey lowered themselves to the floor. Honey looked as though she believed she was going to die. Beckman looked away. He didn't have the courage to face her. His mind raced. If the man meant to kill them, he would do it outside, not in his living room. He had time.

Beckman tensed the muscles in his wrists and hands, remembering from the Cowboys and Indians games of childhood that if he tensed his muscles while he was being tied up, he might be able to pull his hands free after relaxing them. The man tied Honey's hands. Then her feet. She was sobbing.

"Shut up," the man shouted, enraged.

"Please, Mrs. Moskowski, don't make him mad," Beckman pleaded.

The man tied Beckman next, biting the cord into his wrists and ankles.

"That'll hold you till I get back," he said. "And for a long while after." The man left, followed by his dog.

Beckman immediately relaxed his hand and leg muscles and began tugging to free himself, but the cord would not give. He tried, sometimes frantically, until his hands and feet felt swollen and numb. His desperation only seemed to strengthen the cords. He relaxed again, and calmly formed an image of the bindings in his mind. He felt sure this time, even confident. Wasn't he in the very same position that he had described to Dr. Drew? The image of the cords formed with that of his hands and wrists, bound in grotesque and twisted blue shapes. He concentrated on the cords, down into the thread structure, deeper into the fibrous twisting's; down, down into the heart of its molecular chains, its atoms, electrons, protons, and neutrons, and deeper into the level where all energy and matter become one.

The desperate need for his gift began to work. He could no longer see it mentally, but he knew it was working; altering energy levels, separating sub-atomic particles, breaking molecular chains, loosening fibers, the destructive, internal eruption spreading and decaying throughout the cord like a swift-moving disease.

"Beckman! Beckman! God! What's wrong with you? Can't you do something?"

"I'm trying, dammit. I was concentrating. Why did you have to interrupt?"

"Jesus, it's no time for games. For God's sake, do something sensible, something logical."

Beckman ignored her and tried to break the cord once more. He tried concentrating again, but that was gone too. They heard the sound of the Model A outside, then the car door slammed. The man's dog barked, and then the sound of both of them coming up the wooden steps.

The man walked in, leaned his gun against the table, and held the captured prize up by the neck, his one eye gleaming in the yellow lamplight like a small oval mirror. Without a word, the man sat down. He threw his feet up onto the table, leaned back in his chair until it creaked under the strain, and drank, letting the whiskey take him wherever it would. His one eye became dull and it stared, through the light, across the room and beyond.

"I think we've had it," Beckman whispered, but instantly wishing he had not said it.

Honey knew what he meant and looked on with increasing horror. The man continued swilling from the bottle.

They waited for the unknown effect of the whiskey, which came first as a song, something alien and mournful. Beckman could not understand the words. Then they heard maniacal laughter, interspersed by a loud dialogue with a phantom named Febus, and concluding much later in a wild solitary dance around the table until the man stopped, glared into the darkness with his eye, and flopped back into the chair. He wavered for a few moments before passing out, head-first, on the table.

Beckman struggled with renewed desperation at his bonds; pulling, jerking, twisting, when unexpectedly he felt them give, just a little, then more, struggling until he had wiggled a hand free. Quickly he pulled the rest of the cords from his other hand and ankles, then untied Honey, who was breathing the way she had in the back seat of the Model A.

"Quietly now, let's creep out of here."

Honey nodded, disheveling her hair. "The keys," Honey whispered.

Beckman put his finger to his lips. "Go to the car. I'll get them from his pocket. If you'll . . ."

"No way. I'm sticking with you."

"All right, but be very quiet."

Together they tiptoed to the old man. Beckman, with soundless gentility, picked the man up from the table and leaned him upright in the chair, retching at the decayed stench that swam up from his body. The moment Beckman reached into his pocket the man's eye popped open with drunken surprise. Beckman jammed his hand into the man's pocket again, fingers hunting madly for the keys.

The old man opened his mouth, but before he could get anything out, Honey grabbed one of the bones off the table. It was sharp and jagged at one end where it had been broken and gnawed. Holding the rounded joint end and, using the jagged end of the bone as a primitive knife, she jabbed it into the man's one good eye. He yelled a bubbly, underwater type scream and fell backward. Beckman quickly found the keys in the other pocket as the old man twisted in agony on the floor.

Beckman was, strangely, most aware of the drumming their shoes made on the wood floor as they charged, headfirst, out of the house. There seemed an interminable lunging for the car. The starter ground over forever, and it was only after the car started and there seemed to be a chance, did Beckman realize that the old man's dog had torn both of his pants legs off, along with some of his skin. The dog was still outside, leaping repeatedly at the car window.

Beckman shoved the gear lever in reverse and spun the car around. For a moment he caught sight of the old man stumbling, blindly, out of his door, gun in hand and blood covering one side of his face. Beckman pushed the gear lever in low and drove toward the road as fast as the car could take the bumps. The gun started blasting away behind them, and with each blast he and Honey flinched.

Beckman didn't really feel safe until they were back on Interstate 55, which he welcomed with uncontrollable tears. Even the hustling, eighteen-wheel, tractor trailers blasting by him made him delirious with joy. Honey cried and laughed, and impulsively hung her head out of the window, letting the wind blow her hair into wild, Medusan confusion.

She would yell into the wind and breathe deeply. "Oh God, don't you love the smells and the noise? I love it. I love it. Hurry home, Beckman, hurry home."

Beckman, growing more self-conscious of his and Honey's condition, drove quickly into the driveway and into the garage, which was surprisingly empty. "Where is the professor?"

"Oh, I don't know. That isn't important right now, come on." Honey scrambled out of the car, motioning for him to hurry.

"What's the rush?"

"I want to get clean."

"Well, go. I'll wait."

"No, let's get clean together."

She took him by the hand and led the way through the connecting doors of the house, to the bathroom. Beckman felt oddly like an adolescent, being led to his first sin.

"It's a small version of a Roman bath house, copied from Naples. It was largely Leon's doing, but I insisted on the freeform tub. Stimulating, don't you think?"

Tiles with large mosaics, of nude male and female figures in various poses, covered the floor of the bathroom. The room was bordered with multi-colored tile squares. Roman columns supported a shower stall. The fixtures were of assorted erotica—the shower head resembled a limp penis and the hot and cold water knobs young, erect breasts, all done in a smooth, flesh-colored, ceramic material molded over the metal parts.

Honey turned the shower on, adjusted the water as hot as she could stand it. Taking Beckman by both hands, she stepped in with him. The idea of hot water did seem restorative, and he felt the way Honey said she felt. He even echoed her in a kind of sing-song refrain, "I want to get clean, I want to get clean," and it wasn't because of the sex, for he felt no guilt about that, and he knew that Honey didn't. It was rather an attempt, he thought, to clean away the event, the close meeting with an ignominious death; and it would take more water, more heat, more sex to restore life and to switch off the memory.

Honey began to take off her clothes. Beckman followed, realizing with sobering clarity at the same time, that this was his last pair of pants. They were torn to shreds and bloody from the dog bites and where he had cut his leg on something. He dropped his clothes next to Honey's and together they stood under the shower, motionless for a long while, letting the water streak away the blood, the tears, and the heavy dirt from their bodies.

Then, taking a bar of highly scented soap, Beckman gently scrubbed Honey's back, the gleaming hills of her breasts, the two firm little mounds of buttocks, and the soft, fleshy cavern between her legs, alive with sensation—all were washed clean, then anointed with rare perfume. Honey washed Beckman's body, taking care to be delicate and thorough with his genitals.

They moved from the preparatory shower to the sunken tub, which resembled a shallow wading pool, with marble steps descending into clear water. Assorted tropical plants thrived at the other end of the tub, under the white light of a frosted glass skylight. Water ran from a chrome fish's mouth, down a stepped ceramic fall, through the plants and into the bath. It was a restful sound, like a small, isolated waterfall in the tropics. The water was recirculated, if desired, through an opening shaped like a giant uvula in the side of the pool.

Beckman submerged his body and looked across the pool at Honey. She was completely submerged except for her head, which rested on the edge of the pool. Her eyes were closed, and her face had regained its former fullness. The lines had disappeared, and she smiled contentedly.

"Mrs. Moskowski."

She opened her eyes.

"Why isn't the professor here?"

"I don't know. And please, will you call me Honey?"

"Aren't you worried about him finding us?"

"No." She closed her eyes again and sighed.

"Then it must be true?"

Her eyes popped open. "What must be true?"

A pause.

"Hoss says that your husband is a homosexual."

Honey smiled. "He is."

"Then he's . . ."

"After your friend Hoss? I'm sure he is. I'm surprised you didn't notice sooner. Leon had a hard-on for him the minute he saw him. He's got a thing for the rough trade. Tough guys really turn him on."

Beckman sat up abruptly, splashing water over the edge onto the tile figures.

"Oh, don't worry about your friend. He can take care of himself. Besides, Leon never forces anybody, he just pays. Your friend Hoss is probably going to cost him a month's salary."

"Listen, Hoss wouldn't do anything like that."

Honey laughed in an explosive way.

"Maybe not. I've certainly learned something about what I will and will not do in the last twenty-four hours. I know it's a rather worn out cliché, but until last night I really believed money could buy anything." She shuddered. "Oh, I wish to God it would go away."

"Time, give it time," Beckman said, fearing she might go under with a second, more destructive wave of remembering.

"You're strangling with curiosity, aren't you?"

"Not necessarily." Beckman tried to sound indifferent.

"Yes, you are. I know you, you would-be writer and magician. You've got that terminal disease. I can see it wasting you already, so I'll tell you. It might calm my nerves and help me forget.

"It's the old story of the student-teacher thing. Malany and I were students in his class. Leon was a graduate teaching assistant, working for the big PhD. Jesus. Now that I look back at it, it was all such classical textbook stuff. But how can you know the truth until you know what you're looking at? Leon was in the throes of resisting and compensating for his growing homosexuality. I was the cute rich girl from the house on the hill, heavy into toppling the towers of Ilium. You know, doing it with the working class; demonstrating for minority rights during the days, and going down on a selected one at night.

"I even had pictures of me doing it with a black stud to send to my old man, but they got lost somewhere. I don't know. Anyway, I was sort of on the rebound when Leon came at me like a Mack truck. Well, his being Jewish and a future professor was a different kind of turn-on for me. Plus, I'd heard all these stories about how great the Jewish boys were in bed—until then I hadn't made it with one. So, after we'd had the obligatory shack up for a few months, Leon starts talking about marriage. I was getting nowhere in school, and the idea of being the settled-down professor's wife rather appealed to me, so we did it. Lived like Mr. and Mrs. Super Straight for a year. Then, one morning at the breakfast table, Leon drops it on me that he's now a homosexual and has had a steady lover for the last two months."

"Didn't you suspect? I mean, when he couldn't make it in bedroom?"

"Well no, actually. There were periods of impotency during his psychotherapy but other than that, he seemed to enjoy it as much as any man. I asked him about that, and he said he simply thought about fucking some guy that he had the hots for, or he would think about his lover. He even kept a couple of fag magazines hidden so that when all else failed, he would turn on by looking at erotic pictures of men, then give me a quick bang."

"How did that make you feel?"

Honey submerged her entire body—eyes and mouth shut tight—into the warm, circulating water. Beckman waited with some anxiety until she came back up, sweeping her wet hair behind her ears and brushing the water away from her eyes.

"Let's say I learned a few things about myself. Up to then I thought I could tolerate anything, another woman, okay, but a man, a homosexual, a fag, I felt like a complete fool. I screamed and threw things. Leon kept dodging the plates and apologizing. It was like something out of a porn comic strip.

"Then, suddenly, I realized that I was free. I mean really free. Not just divorced free, but free of any trace of emotional commitment, or repercussions, or any goddamn thing. We, quite coldly, I might add, worked out an arrangement. We would maintain the appearances of marriage so that Leon could keep his public deniability, and we could both be free to have lovers, to do anything we wanted so long as it didn't openly jeopardize the other."

Beckman shook his head. "It must be really tough. I mean, don't you miss never being in love?"

Honey looked genuinely puzzled. "I don't know what you mean. I'm in love all the time."

"Never mind," Beckman said. "Does Malany know about this?"

Honey laughed. "Hell, no. Poor kid. She is so fucked up, going around half dazed all the time, writing those silly poems. She really believes in that stuff, going to be another Edna St. Vincent Millay."

"I thought you were friends," Beckman said.

"We are, but you can only have so much sympathy." Beckman looked puzzled. Honey clearly saw that further explanation was necessary. "I think she could have done better by staying at home with her husband," she continued. "But she had to take off, live like a vagabond poetess, starve, freeze, the whole suffering bit, and then to go with that vanity publisher. Christ, I'll bet that cost her husband a good jolt . . ."

Honey continued talking. Beckman watched her lips move, her expression change. She was a good actress, keenly aware of her face and hands. He tried to appear interested, and she seemed not to immediately notice the changes coming over him. A fierce ringing in his head silenced the outside world, and he was afraid that his body would crumple under the near perfect vacuum that it had become.

Honey stopped talking and looked at him strangely. Beckman allowed himself to slip under the water, into a not-so-quiet world of bubbles and gurgles, of blood pounding in his ears and the creak of tight muscles holding down air. He considered suicide, but he didn't think of it as suicide at the time. It was more like some sweet and wonderful voice had whispered "relief, peace and solitude" in his ear. Just the words whispered softly, like a mother's promise. It wasn't even painful holding his breath, but just in case his body refused to go along, he tried to edge his head into the great sculptured uvula, feeling at once the water being drawn swiftly past his head. His hair lurched straight into the cavity. There was, for a few moments, a pleasant sensation of falling, just gently tumbling through a tunnel lit with sparkling lights of red and blue and green. Then, although he wasn't truly aware of it at the time, he was drawn, with almost painful violence, from the uvula up to the surface.

"What the hell do you think you're doing?" Honey shouted.

Beckman laughed. "Trying to return to the safety of the womb in your bathtub. Why?"

"Jesus. Because of what I told you about Malany? You mean Malany got to you like that? Christ almighty, I'm glad I didn't tell you about it when that smelly Cyclops had the gun on us. You might have let him eat us."

"I might have," Beckman said, laughing. He continued laughing until his face turned purple and the vein in his forehead stood out like a heavy rope covered in thin plastic. He laughed, pounded the water with his hands, and thrashed it around like a frenzied child.

Honey got out of the tub, wrapped herself in a large towel, and sat on one of the marble benches near the edge. She waited, legs crossed, chin resting in her hand until Beckman's seizure subsided, and he lay in the churning, rippling water, quiet and resigned.

"What was it, Beckman? The dark soul, the unapproachableness, the irresistible appearance of a literary mind, or all of it? That's what seeped its way into the core of your pampered self, isn't it?"

Beckman did not answer.

"Oh well, it doesn't matter. You're really lucky. A lesson in reality didn't cost you a dime. Think of her poor husband."

"She has a husband?" Beckman asked and immediately thought of the man he had seen her with at the bookstore. "Who is he?" Beckman demanded.

"Don't act totally stupid, Beckman. Get out of the water. You're starting to look ridiculous."

Honey rose abruptly from the bench, towel still draped over her body in terrycloth folds.

"Come on. Let's go to the bedroom. We can get dressed or we can have a celebration of life, whatever you want."

Beckman pushed himself out of the water. For a long while he stood frozen in Honey's gaze as the bathwater ran off his body and formed a spreading pool at his feet. Honey handed him a towel, letting her hand rub across his buttocks.

"Who is he, Mrs. Moskowski?"

Honey rolled her eyes.

"Oh, I don't really know. I've never met him, but Malany tells me he's rich, he's in the investment business, in his mid-fifties, and for some completely unfathomable reason, worships at her feet."

Beckman followed Honey up the stairs to her bedroom which had an adjoining bath, both furnished and decorated in Louis XIV style.

"All originals," she was quick to add. "I've left this chair unrestored." She motioned casually toward a delicately lined chair, covered with faded red upholstery, woven with patterns of dancing unicorns. The gold leaf on the wood had almost vanished, but enough remained so that the effect of pure elegance was still there.

If the craftsman didn't believe in the divine right of kings, he knew how to convince his royal patron that he did.

"Wait here," Honey said, stepping into the adjoining bathroom and closing the door behind her. Beckman felt a cold shiver ripple through his body. He rubbed himself with the towel until parts of his skin felt raw. He understood now why Malany had never appeared to need money—and the black Lincoln. The man he saw in the bookstore with her must be her husband. He had followed her across the country, dropping white envelopes stuffed with money whenever she needed them. Why didn't she tell him? It would not have mattered that she was married. What did matter, and what now angered him, were the appearances she presented.

The struggling poetess trying to make it on her own, rejecting the good and warm things of life so that she could write. Beckman had respected her for that above all else. The sincerity, the self-denial, the radicalism and the determination had all been an illusion that she had called, with conviction, "reality."

Beckman dropped down on the edge of Honey's bed, tears running from his eyes.

"Here, cut that out, I can't use it," Honey said.

She stood before him, naked except for the columnar white wig worn by the ladies of Louis XVI's court. His eyes immediately traveled to the black nevus pasted on her right thigh. Before he fully realized it, his nose was only a few inches from the delicate, oval indention of her navel and while his tongue explored its beautiful wonders, she quickly arranged a powdered white wig on his head. He started to laugh at the image of himself sitting on the edge of a football-field-sized bed, covered in a body towel like a lecherous Roman senator, wearing a George Washington wig, and staring into the navel of one of Marie Antoinette's ladies-in-waiting.

He laughed even as she pushed his face into the delicate softness of her belly and held him there so that his laughing sounded like continuous baby farts, and continued as she pushed him down through the crisp tangle of pubic hairs, on down to the opened gates where all of humanity has, and will forever, enter the world.

There he lingered, in the fleeting and impossible hope of finding transformation from the irrevocable physicalness of life. Honey, sensing his desire, pushed and thrust, pushed and thrust until Beckman, overcome with even greater lust, injected the mad tentacle of his tongue and with it searched the mysteries of her womanhood.

Only a few hours ago, Beckman could count on two fingers the times he'd had sexual intercourse. The first was the game of guilt-ridden coitus interruptus he and his high school girlfriend had played the night after a football game. They had swilled a whole six-pack of beer and had cheered their team on to victory in the state tournament. It was done in the quiet of a necropolis where they parked her parent's car and, with fear and trembling, exposed the forbidden fruits. It was, as he was to learn later, like most first encounters among the innocent and the ignorant—clumsy, painful, terrifying, and not a little ridiculous. It never happened with her again, and only a short time after that she stopped speaking to him completely.

The second time was with a prostitute twice his age who bore the scars of a radical mastectomy, a butchered appendectomy, and a difficult Caesarean. That was shortly after he had moved into his first apartment, over a bar in east Baltimore. She was sitting at the bar discussing *Brave New World*. Beckman was feeling highly gregarious and free-spirited. He sat next to the woman and immediately joined the conversation. The possibility that she was a prostitute had never occurred to him. He assumed she was a public school teacher, relaxing after a tough day with the school kids and, he found out later, that was what she actually had been, but had to resign over "some trouble." He couldn't remember exactly how it happened, or just when she unveiled the truth, but Beckman, after seeing her paunchy, scarred body and the lined, sagging face in the light from his window, watched his drunken erection shrink like a deflating balloon. Observing this, the prostitute announced that he needed a "Frenchie," whereupon he experienced, for the first time, the unheard-of practice—except in jokes—of fellatio. The prostitute worked for over thirty minutes, using all of her anatomical knowledge, but with only partial success. Almost in desperation, and as a last resort, she began a mild, erotic dance about the room, resembling a naked belly dancer, pumping her hips, fondling her one breast and culminating in an act simulating orgasm.

Beckman had read from authorities on the subject that sex was purely a mental phenomenon. There had been case studies on mentally retarded adults to back it up, studies on psychotics, neurotics, asexuals, homosexuals, and classical heterosexuals of average intelligences—all supporting the hypothesis of the psychological dependency of sexual dysfunction. So, Beckman was completely mystified to see his erection reestablished, at least firm enough to do the job, while mentally he felt nothing but revulsion and disgust with his situation. The prostitute, seeing her efforts as successful, leapt into Beckman's bed and motioned for him to hurry. Beckman, with servile obedience, did as he was bid until sufficient time had gone by, when he joined the prostitute in faking an orgasm.

# CHAPTER 15

Lying in bed with the sleeping Mrs. Moskowski, his body drained of its seminal fluids, his ubiquitous symbol of creation and vitality lying raw and withered as a flailed piece of rope on his leg, he felt mystified and slightly appalled at the situation he now found himself in. His George Washington wig had twisted during sleep so that its pigtail hung over his ear. Even Honey's wig had fallen off and lay like an empty beehive beside her. A year ago, before his last birthday, he would have recoiled from this crazy scene. He would have struggled with the sadness of it for days. But now it was as if a rush-hour crowd had pushed him aside, declaring him forever invalid, denying him their reasons, and their purpose. He felt adrift without wanting to be, forced against his will to find separate reasons and, if he was extremely lucky, a new purpose.

The feeling depressed him and the painful dryness in his throat reminded him of his mortal, ever aging body. He slipped out of bed, wincing from the pain in his genitals, and walked, bowlegged as a rodeo cowboy, to the bathroom. He turned the water on in the shower as hot as he could stand it, and stepped in, determined to bear the pain in the tenderest of places, until the water had numbed it.

He had done some reading on alpha therapy when he started into psychokinesis, so while the hot water coursed over his body, he tried to see only pleasant scenes; mental gray and white pictures of ocean waves on the beach, or gulls turning and calling over Baltimore's inner harbor, but his efforts were shattered when Honey flung the shower curtain aside and stepped in.

"Ouch, how can you stand it?"

Beckman simply didn't feel like answering. He truly didn't give a damn, until she reached for his tortured organ.

"Not!" He leapt back, banging his head against the shower wall.

"Ooooh," Honey cooed, "it's hurt, poor thing. Well, I hope it recovers by tomorrow." She picked up the soap and started to wash her body, smiling at Beckman's predicament. "Let's go out tonight. I have the most wonderful place I want to take you."

"Mrs. Moskowski, I'm broke, not a dime."

"Christ, don't worry about it. It's on me."

"I can't. I just . . . "

"Oh, don't let your dated masculine pride get in the way. Besides, I probably owe you a great deal for saving my life."

"I really didn't do anything. If you hadn't put that guy's eye out . . . "

"Don't talk about it, don't even think about it." Honey looked like a greased-up English Channel swimmer.

"Mrs. Moskowski, I want to find out what's happened to Malany."

"Let's don't discuss it, all right? And for God's sake, will you please call me Honey!" She screamed her name loud enough to momentarily deafen him.

"Okay, all right. There's no need to get angry."

"I'm not angry. It's just that I can't stand to be called that, especially by you. I have to take it from Leon's hypocritical colleagues. Oh, those verbose clods are real masters of convoluted duplicity."

"And the poet?" Beckman asked.

"Ha, the greatest lying lecher of them all."

"So, his interest in Malany is all phony?"

"I'll say. If he's had any luck at all, she's probably been deflowered more times than you have."

Beckman stepped out of the shower and, dripping wet, went straight into the bedroom to dress.

"What the hell do you think you can do, punch him out like some spurned and outraged lover? Malany does what she wants to do, you should know that. He's a satyr, that's true, but he's not a rapist. If he makes it with her, it'll be with her consent. So, what are you going to do?"

Beckman stopped, stared straight ahead with pinpoint pupils, past Honey, through the wall, unaware that his underclothes had become soaked with water.

"Here," Honey said, tossing him last night's only unsoiled towel. "Finish drying, I want to take you out."

Beckman thought his lack of fascination, or even of curiosity, with the assorted degenerates of Honey's private club might indicate a rapidly maturing attitude of tolerance, or could it mean that he was on the road to what the female impersonator sitting at their table called "meaningful fulfillment"? Nothing at Honey's club was what it appeared to be. Even he, at her near tearful insistence, had dressed in a pinstriped, double-breasted suit of the thirties, wore a carnation in the lapel, and had reluctantly pasted his hair back so that he looked like an Esquire whiskey ad of 1933.

He didn't even object when one of Honey's friends, dressed in a black body suit with *DEATH* stenciled in luminous paint across her forehead, joined them, and at once began caressing his leg. He simply took out one of Honey's joints, lit it from the lighted end of the one that she was smoking, and made it a point to ignore the advance.

Honey rambled on with anyone who sat down at her table: nonsense stuff inspired by chain-smoked joints, and dry champagne laced with a drug she called XYZ. They watched, indifferently, a one act play of nude lesbians dramatize their condition in the straight world with a dialogue of screams and curses. Then a chorus line of female and male impersonators, some in futuristic costumes of clear plastic, others dressed like Roman generals.

At the middle point of the show Honey announced that she was bored and wanted to go. No one seemed to notice even though she had shouted it at the top of her voice. Beckman followed her, weaving past groups of large-muscled, African big game hunters, and assorted historical figures in cod pieces, out to the car. She put a finger to his chin with unusually hard pressure.

"You drive, please."

Honey was more than drunk. She was high, in the broadest sense of the word. It was as though her mind raced out of control and her body now functioned strictly on hyperfine stimuli. She seemed like a totally rational, completely alert, extra-planetary creature.

Beckman drove her home, which she seemed not to recognize. He sat up with her while she babbled continuous nonsense, drank from a fresh bottle of vodka, and searched, with periodic hysteria, for her lost cocaine. It was after four a.m. before she finally toppled over and Beckman dragged her to bed, made sure she was safe, then removed her keys and a $20 bill from her purse.

He had managed to wangle the poet's address from Honey before her awareness checked out. It was a seventh story apartment downtown, overlooking the Mississippi River and the Arkansas flats, with inspiring sunsets when the sky was clear. Beckman parked Honey's Model A across the street from the apartment building. He waited, feeling like a 1920s mobster. A few lights shone on the seventh story. Were they the poet's? Beckman had forgotten to get the poet's apartment number. He got out of the car, which, as in

1928, still required some elegance, and glanced ominously down to both ends of the light dotted street.

He dashed, catlike, to the building entrance, and stepped back against the wall, out of the glow of the streetlight. He felt completely ridiculous and, as he kept asking himself; what the hell was he going to do? Rescue Malany as though she were some damsel in distress, or had Honey's grass and booze turned him into a temporary psychotic?

Car lights turned toward him, moving down the street. Beckman pressed himself flatter against the wall and tried to think of a believable story in case it was the police. The car rolled slowly by. It was the black Lincoln.

Beckman gripped the wall with all ten fingers. He could see the driver looking at the entrance door. The Lincoln went past him and parked in the first space beyond the no parking zone in front of the building. Beckman watched, almost hypnotized by the glaring red taillights of the car. The thought of meeting Malany's husband face to face, at four thirty in the morning and in front of the apartment building where she had, he suspected, broken her ascetic vows, made him slightly dizzy.

The driver stepped quietly out of the car and started walking toward him. It was the same big man he saw talking to her in the old man's bookstore. It was clear to Beckman that he would undoubtedly end up, if he was lucky, in the hospital if the man chose to be unreasonable. The man passed him. Without consciously intending it, Beckman moved behind the man and shoved his finger in the man's back, grabbing him by the collar at the same time. The man froze and Beckman, encouraged, pushed the man's face against the wall.

"Okay, buddy, don't shoot. Don't shoot. You can have it—all I got." The man pleaded.

To Beckman's disappointment, the man was trembling; trembling hard enough to rattle the change in his pocket.

"Who are you?" Beckman asked, trying to disguise his voice.

"Look, I'm a private investigator, just trying to do a job. That's all."

"Well, what are you doing driving that car?"

"It was part of the expense deal. Hey, who are you? Why do you want to know all this?" The man stopped shaking and was glancing back.

Beckman couldn't think of a believable explanation, especially since he couldn't think of one that wasn't a lie. He continued the bluff, backing away slowly, and said, in his most deadly voice, "Don't move or else."

At that, the man dropped his hands and spun around.

Beckman ran for the car. He could hear, even feel, the man's heavy footfalls behind him. There was no time for psychokinetic concentration. He merely wished, with all of his racing heart, that the man would fall and possibly break his leg. Beckman jumped in the Model A, locked the door, and ground the slow-starting engine while the huge man outside ripped away the door handle and pounded the window glass into webbed fractures.

"I know you, buddy, and you can bet this'll be in my report!"

The engine started and the Model A leapt clumsily away from the curb, leaving the private investigator stumbling forward in a delayed fall to the street. Beckman drove through the streets of Memphis, panic stricken. He drove without direction or plan, without reasoning, until the car clanked and sputtered with its last drop of fuel. He coasted silently to a stop beside a vast darkness. An unlighted necropolis? No one wastes light on the dead. He was lost, out of fuel, and still not safe. He curled up in the front seat and waited for morning. There seemed little else to do. Morning would come with its perennial promise of a new start.

Beckman awoke with a start and, for a few moments, did not remember where he was. It always frightened him when this happened, and he sat up quickly. A stiffening pain shot down his neck and back. His legs were cramped but, surprisingly, he had slept.

There wasn't a hint as to what time it was. Beckman wished that he had not hocked his watch last year to buy a case of Muscatel. He needed to know what time it was. He needed that solid and enduring handhold on reality.

A green and thickly wooded park appeared from the vast grayness of morning. Waist-high mist floated among its still-life energy. Beckman got out of the car and looked around. Inconspicuous residential homes jammed the opposite side of the street, and there wasn't a gas station in sight, or a telephone. He noticed a movement in the park, and watched as a woman, dressed in a white robe, emerged out of the mist. Seeing him, she turned and ran, almost seeming to float away from him.

"Wait!" Beckman shouted. "Wait! I only want to ask you something!"

The woman ran on, robe flowing behind, and mist swirling in her wake. The ground was spongy, and Beckman sank as he lost traction in the soggy, grassy ground. He tried, but he could not close the distance. Was it the condition of the ground or was the woman a true spirit? He was afraid that she might vanish at any moment. But she didn't vanish. Instead she abruptly stopped and turned to face him. Beckman slowed his pace to catch his breath. The woman was young with wide, clear gray eyes and long, light hair.

"I'm not going to bother you. I only want to know what time it is. I'm lost and out of gas."

The woman continued to stare at him. She had not heard or understood a word of what he had said.

"Look, please believe me. I'm not going to hurt you. If you don't know what time it is, then could you tell me where I am and where I can get some gas?"

Yellow sunlight split through the trees and refracted in the mist, glowing around the girl in rainbow colors. Her image seemed to blur and fade into transparency. Beckman, believing now that he was seeing the vision he had longed for since childhood, fell to his knees, sinking several inches into the wet ground.

"Don't go away, please. I'm lost. I need to know what time it is. Please help me."

The woman, trembling a little, looked at her watch. "It's six—si—si—six thirty, mister. Please, mister, don't hurt me. I'm just a secretary. Please don't mess with me. I won't tell anybody. Please."

Beckman rose from the ground. Cold water ran down his lower legs. The knees of his pants were caked with black mud.

"You mean you're not . . ."

"I'm not crazy, mister, really I'm not. I just like to come out here sometimes before work and walk around. It's real nice this time of morning. I know you think I'm crazy, but I'm not. Really."

"But I thought, I hoped you would help me."

"Help you?"

"Yes," Beckman said.

The woman looked at her watch again. "Uh, it's 6:35 now, mister, and I don't know where the nearest gas station is, but I'll be glad to call somebody for you when I go to work."

The girl started backing away, slowly.

"Jesus, how I had wished, how I had hoped, you were from another place, a spirit, an angel, or even an alien from another planet."

"Oh, God!" the woman half-screamed, throwing her hands to her mouth before she dashed past Beckman and ran, hard, toward the street.

Beckman thought of running after her, but the effort seemed like everything he had tried since meeting Malany—pointless. He could find his way back to Honey's with a little extra trouble. He wasn't really convinced that the woman was not truly crazy. He now had the comfortable assurance of facts. The woman was a secretary; the time was 6:35. He walked back to the car, ankle-deep in wet grass and mud. The sun was higher and most of the mist had evaporated, exposing pockets of litter.

He trudged on to the car and down the street. A twisted sign labeled it Goodlett Ave. and, several blocks down, he found a gas station attendant not too eager to sell him a gallon of their precious liquid.

Strangely, he was not far from Honey's home. Perhaps there had been a calmer reasoning voice whispering directions to him during his escape. He recognized some of the houses. He knew that a large golf course was nearby. They were the only truths of his past, his recent past that he carried with him from last night. Malany, Hoss, California—all were far away and receding into infinity.

Beckman parked Honey's Model A beside the professor's car. The Model A was splattered with mud and rain streaked. He made as little noise as possible. He touched the hood of the professor's car; still warm, tinkling sounds came from the cooling metal. He entered the house through the back way but had to stop. He couldn't ignore the sounds of weeping from the living room. He peeked around the door.

The professor was huddled against Honey's shoulder, sobbing. Honey, embracing him, patted his back and whispered cooing baby words next to his ear. The professor blubbered something about love and unimaginable cruelty, and Honey cooed in his ear some more. Then, almost as if someone had interrupted this scene to whisper the fact of Beckman's presence, she looked up straight at him, and signaled with her eyes for him to go upstairs.

Beckman turned and started up the steps, no longer caring about remaining inconspicuous. He consciously stomped up the stairs and, bursting into Honey's room, began gathering up his few belongings.

After a few minutes, Honey stormed into the room and watched in disbelief as Beckman stuffed the last of his underwear into his duffle bag.

"What are you doing?" she half screamed.

"Going to California." Beckman was calm and decisive.

"And what do you expect to find when you get there, the end of the rainbow?"

"It's beginning to look that way."

"Well, good luck. But the Pacific Ocean is very cold, believe me."

"You've been there, I suppose?" Beckman snapped. He was breaking down.

"Of course. I went there when it was fashionable to leave home and find yourself."

"And did you?"

"Oh, sure. After paying out enough to buy yachts for two shrinks and one sex counselor who wanted to put her hypotheses into practice with me. I found out that I knew what I was all along. I've had to fake the phony morality bit occasionally. People expect it, you know, especially when they feel threatened."

"What about that scene with your husband?"

"Leon's just a child, a lollipop-sucking child, only now its phalluses. He needs babying, occasionally, when he's had a disappointment."

"Did he see Hoss?"

"That, I should say, he did," she said.

"And what does 'that' mean?"

"Well, Leon says he took Malany's car and invited him to go with him to New Orleans. Your friend, Hoss, spent most of his time there drinking and throwing away the rest of his money, or was it his money? Anyway. According to Leon, your friend was very cooperative. He must have had a good line; poor Leon's heart is broken."

Beckman swung the duffle bag over his shoulder and angrily waved his finger in front of Honey's face.

"I'm getting out of here. You people are all crazy, and I think you're all dangerous." Beckman started for the door.

"Okay, go to California and jump in the Pacific Ocean for all I care. But remember, you'll be doing it alone. Nobody here will give a shit, especially Malany. She'll be too busy going down on John Darling."

Beckman stopped and slowly turned. "You're really a witch, aren't you? I mean, you're a real case study in pure evil."

"Only when I want something. I can be what you call evil. And, for the moment, I want you, Beckman. It's been wonderful with you. Don't go, not now. Stay a little longer. I can get Malany back for you, and then you can go."

Beckman let his duffle bag slip to the floor. He had not really wanted to leave. The thought of going without her had become physically painful. The end would come with the last drop of their desire. There was nothing now but to feed from the great mound of their flesh. They fell toward each other, groping, grasping, fumbling with his mechanical fasteners; not waiting or caring, but using any convenient platform, first the floor, then the bed. Beckman and Honey, in total surrender to the alternating agony and ecstasy of sensual infinity, seemed to rattle the very windows with the dissonant trills of orgasm.

# CHAPTER 16

It was about three in the morning when Hoss woke up, still dazed from the alcohol and marijuana. He started to roll out of bed but felt the body of a woman next to him. He searched his memory but could not recall meeting her or sleeping with her. He couldn't recall having sex either, but from the condition of the bed and his flaccid member, it was obvious that he had.

The streetlight outside the window illumined the room sufficiently to allow him to find his clothes. He slipped on his soiled shirt and tried putting on his pants standing up. This was a mistake, since he quickly lost his balance and hopped around on one foot, while the other foot was wedged in the left pants leg. He couldn't prevent crashing into pieces of unseen furniture and nearly slipped on something soft and wet. He finally managed to slide his pants over his waist and secure them with his belt. He pulled on his Harley Davidson T-shirt, still reeking of beer and bourbon. He looked at the woman again. She was lying on her back, her mouth gaped open and emitting grunting sounds from her throat. Her blonde wig had slipped off her head, revealing a matted pelt of thinning gray hair. The blonde wig lay in a tangled mass next to her right ear.

Hoss tried to remember her name but nothing came except a fading kaleidoscope of images from the night before. An urgent need to escape came over him. He felt in his pockets and they were empty, even of the soiled and spotted handkerchief he kept stuffed there. He looked at the woman's purse on the night table next to her bed. Ordinarily, he wouldn't allow himself to think of it, but he was completely out of funds—not a dime was left over from his generosity of the night.

He moved slowly at first, then much quicker once he had committed himself. He unsnapped the woman's purse and felt around in its dark interior. Surprisingly, he discovered Malany's car keys. He withdrew them as though he were pulling a fish out of the water. Then he deftly removed her wallet and searched its interior with his fingers. $200 was all he could find. He wouldn't take the credit cards, just the cash. The $200 would be enough to get him back to Memphis. He slipped the bills into his pocket and eased out the door.

He had failed to lock the doors on Malany's car and did not notice the man sleeping in the backseat. He started the engine and immediately shifted the gear lever into drive, which made him cringe since he had been taught from his first day of driving to always let a cold engine warm up.

He had driven several blocks, not knowing where he was or how to find his way to Memphis when the man in the backseat awakened and sat up directly behind Hoss, who noticed him instantly from the rearview mirror. Hoss presently stopped breathing.

"Whor in the fuck did you come from?" he shouted.

The man had all the appearance of someone washed up on a beach, still covered in his torn and wrinkled clothes.

"Where are we going?" The man asked looking bewildered.

Hoss pulled the car next to the curb and stopped, leaving the engine idling.

"We ain't goin' no place!" Hoss shouted. "Get out! Get outta here now!"

The man reached for the door with a look of terror on his dirt-streaked face.

"Wait!" Hoss shouted again. "Wait!"

The man froze, his hand still on the door handle. He stared straight ahead as though waiting for the executioner's axe to fall.

"How much you know about this town?" Hoss asked.

"Pretty much everything. I was born and raised here. Know every street and alley, every stone and secret, know things that haven't happen yet."

"Da ya know how to get to Memphis from here?"

"Just go straight down this street until you see the signs to Interstate 55 North, then take the off ramp and it'll take you straight to Memphis." There was a long hesitation, and then the man said. "Can I go with ya? I won't be any trouble. I promise. I just want to get out of this evil place."

Hoss did not answer for a long time. Then he said, "You want to go to California?"

"Isn't that the place where they say dreams come true?"

"Yes, that's the place. You got any dreams you want to come true?"

The man thought for a while, then absentmindedly started chewing his fingernails.

"I had dreams once. I had lots of dreams, but none of them came to fruition. I tried, I tried as hard as I could, but . . ."

The man stopped midsentence as though mentally transported to another time.

After a short while, Hoss saw the road sign to I-55 North. He looked back at the man for a moment and said, "Are you sure you want to do this?"

"Yeah, man. Let's do it. I'm not leaving anything behind here except pain and disillusionment."

# CHAPTER 17

John Darling had been a great disappointment to Malany. She spent about a week with him hoping for poetic enlightenment. She had even broken her vow of renewed chastity hoping he would have an emotional breakthrough, but the only thing he seemed to be able to produce was one dry martini after another. Malany had never found acute alcoholism alluring or productive. Smoking grass was, in her thinking, a far better stimulant of the imagination.

She left after about a week. Darling was asleep or unconscious—she couldn't decide which—in bed. She called a cab and waited outside on the edge of the street until the cab came. Honey's house felt cool and refreshing and, after the self-degradation she had gone through with Professor Darling, she realized she needed a shower. A shower usually made her feel spiritually and physically clean, but after the shower she continued to feel like she was coated with a thin layer of slime. She put on clean clothes thinking that would dampen her sense of shame—it didn't. She wandered into Honey's library. Honey had an extensive collection of all the great writers from ancient to modern including Chinese and Japanese. Malany selected a volume of poetry by Allen Ginsburg, *Howl.* She had met Ginsburg once. She had gone to a poetry reading while she was an undergraduate. Afterward her Literature professor, Dr. Moseros, invited her to a party where Ginsburg would be a guest. He was a rather short, balding man, thick-set with thick round glasses. He showed little interest in talking to her or anyone at the party. He simply wanted to know where the bathrooms and telephone were. She remembered being a little upset that he did not seem to recognize her as a fellow poet.

She tried reading *Howl*, but the text seemed more like the ravings of a mad man, barely coherent and disassociated; not the musings of a sensitive poet. She put the book down, determined to pick it up and try again. She tried writing but found herself staring out of the window much of the time. She decided to look into her own past writing to see if she could pick up a few loose verbal stings. She leafed through her *Song and Saber* but to her horror the words seemed meaningless, aesthetically void and pretentious. She threw her book across the room and watched it as it crashed against the shelves of Honey's library and fluttered to the floor like a wounded bird. She quickly found her way to Honey's liquor cabinet and poured a large glass of vodka.

Hoss did not realize that Malany would be in the house. He had convinced himself that she was still living with John Darling.

"What are you doing here?" Malany yelled as she looked up and saw Hoss and his new companion walk into the house. "And who is that?"

"This here is Mr. Lockjaw."

"Don't be ridiculous, Hoss. No one is named Lockjaw. He looks like a bum, and he stinks."

"Yes, he is a bum—they call 'em homeless now—but he wants to change his life, follow his dreams. You know, just like you and Beckman—nothing wrong with that, is there?"

"Then why are you here?"

"I come to return your car, maybe take a shower, get something to eat, you know, live like a civilized human being for a day or so," Hoss said.

"I think taking a shower is a good idea for both of you. Why don't you both hurry it up?"

"Mr. Lockjaw here don't have any clothes except what he's got on," Hoss said. "Do you suppose he could borrow some of the professor's? He'll send 'em back, I swear he will."

"Sure," Malany said. "Just go in the closet and select what you want. I'm sure the professor will be happy to loan you some of his sartorial best."

Mr. Lockjaw smiled, showing his dark and encrusted teeth. Malany lead them to the master bathroom, pointing out the various white, fluffy linens and towels. Hoss went first, and Malany told Mr. Lockjaw to follow her. She led him into the library, pointed to the reading chair, picked up *Howl* from the floor and handed it to him.

"If this means anything to you, then you can have it."

Mr. Lockjaw took the book gently and held it in a kind of reverence much like a devout Christian holds the bible or a rabbi holds the Torah. Malany left him and he was carefully opening the cover and turned over the first page. She returned to the guest room where she had been sleeping, picked up her box of *Song and Sabers* and, with some difficulty, carried them downstairs and out to the large, open fire pit that the professor used to roast meat. She, without hesitating, tossed the box into the pit. She then found a plastic container of charcoal lighter fluid, emptied the container onto the books and set it on fire. She watched unmoved as the fire burned and crinkled the books and cardboard box into a small pile of ash. She watched even as the fire started to subside and continued to watch until the last ember had snuffed out. Then, when the last swirls of smoke disappeared into the air, she turned to find Hoss standing behind her.

He had a puzzled expression on his face. "Why did you do that?"

"I had an epiphany, and they are usually destructive."

"A what?" Hoss asked.

"Let's just say I realized some terrible truths about myself."

She walked past Hoss and into the house. Mr. Lockjaw was standing in the middle of the living room, clean-shaven and wearing one of Leon's best suits.

"Blue becomes you," Malany said. "Why don't you help yourself to one or two of his tweed jackets? He won't miss them."

Mr. Lockjaw smiled and, although he had brushed his teeth, they remained dark and encrusted.

"Hoss," Malany said, turning to him. "Tell me something." She didn't wait for him to respond. "Why did you take Leon with you to New Orleans? I don't get it. I thought you were homophobic."

Hoss chewed his bottom lip for a moment, his eyes shifting from side to side. "Homo what?"

"It's someone who doesn't like homosexuals," Malany said.

"I don't dislike them people, hell, I don't give a shit about 'em. I just don't want them shoving it in my face," Hoss laughed. "I don't care if they shove it in somebody else's, though—know what I mean." He laughed harder now.

"I spoke to Beckman last week on the phone. Leon thinks you're a repressed homosexual."

"A repressed what?" Hoss's face tightened.

"That's someone who denies certain feelings they have," Malany said.

"I ain't a repressed nothing!" Hoss growled. "I just took him along because he's kind of a smart guy and I wanted the company. He knows how I feel about cock suckers. I had come back drunk from some bar on Bourbon Street, flopped on the bed, and passed out. Woke up about three in the morning and that little faggot had my pants down and was going to town on my willy."

"And what did you do—kick the crap out of him?" Malany said, not bothering to conceal her contempt.

"No, I was too drunk and too tired, so I thought what the hell, and let him finish. Next day I told him to get out. The last I saw of him he was getting in a cab—the sneaky little cock sucker."

"Just wanted to clear that up," Malany said with a slight smile.

"Malany," Hoss said, looking down at his feet. "I know we don't get along and all that, but I was wondering if you might loan me your car for about a week or so? I'll get it back to you, I swear." There was a long silence except for the wind. The wind had increased in the last half hour. It whistled around the house and rattled the tree leaves. Malany did not like wind. It always frightened her. There was something in it that threatened madness or doom.

"Tell you what, Hoss, you can have the thing. I won't need it anymore," she said in a tone of resignation.

Hoss looked at her as though he had just been told that he had won the grand prize.

"No shit!" he said.

"No shit," Malany answered.

"What are you going to do now?" Hoss asked.

"I'm going to rejoin my husband, stop kidding myself, and accept the good life he is offering me."

Malany noticed Mr. Lockjaw standing behind Hoss. He was holding several articles of clothing in his right arm and gripping the copy of *Howl* with his other hand close to his chest.

"How do you like the book?" she asked him.

Mr. Lockjaw looked lovingly at the book. "I think it's a brilliant work—a real tour de force."

"And you, Hoss, what are you going to do?"

"Me? I'm going to California."

# CHAPTER 18

Beckman did not like the Gold Coast of Florida. In no way had it lived up to his fantasies of loincloth freedom and paradisiacal plenty. It was, instead, an unnaturally expensive wedge of real estate, overcrowded with assorted rich people, hurrying merchants, and servile domestics, all sealed away by stone, and all speaking a polyglot of dialects from across North America.

It was, however, quieter in Palm Beach than it was in Miami. The elite like their distance, especially from each other and their dogs. Beckman felt he could tolerate the place as long as Honey could, and there was, he had to admit, a certain rare, wasteful elegance in sitting by the pool, in the sun, and drinking coconut milk and vodka from coconut shells mounted in silver holders, then making love to exhaustion at night.

Last night was not to be repeated, at least not by the pool, but in a hot sleeping bag. That had been another of Honey's games. She was Maria and Beckman was Robert Jordan, complete with rifle, wineskin, and beret. They drank over a quart of wine before crawling into the sleeping bag. Beckman had a difficult time being serious, and an even more difficult time trying to pry Honey out of her Spanish Army battle fatigues. The dialogue was to be strictly Hemingwayesque, but the most trying part for Beckman was sex all night, until Honey was satisfied that the earth had moved in the backyard of her Palm Beach home.

Beckman was simply weary, emptied of body and soul. He finished what remained of the concoction in the coconut shell and placed it slowly, carefully, in its silver holder. His body felt pleasantly aflame; internally from the vodka and externally from the sun which had, unnoticed by him, passed its zenith, leaving his flesh smelling something like warm meat.

He rose from the lounge chair and adjusted his jock strap, which was not required dress around the pool but had proven necessary for protection against the sun. He eased into the pool water. It was cool and clear and Beckman, fascinated by the patterns of reflected light dancing on the bottom, didn't see the professor walking toward him until the he was standing directly over him.

The professor had a new companion, a young sailor, an enlisted man, on liberty from a visiting ship. The young sailor, holding his hat respectfully in his hands, gazed around in wonder at the pool. The professor placed his hand familiarly on the sailor's back.

"Beckman, I want you to meet Todd. Todd's one of our young warriors. Aren't you, Todd?"

The sailor was embarrassed. "Well, sir, I wouldn't put it like that."

"Modesty. Don't you think that modesty in a young warrior is irresistible, Beckman?"

"Leon, you know I wouldn't think of it that way."

"Of course not." The professor turned, flashing Beckman a haughty profile, and started straightening the sailor's collar, which had wrinkled in a gust of wind. The sailor appeared confused, yet something about his reluctance warned Beckman that he knew what was going on.

"How is the water?" asked the professor.

"Just great. Very refreshing."

Turning to Todd, the professor asked, "Would you like to go for a swim?"

"Well—yes, if it's all right," the sailor said quietly.

"Then help yourself. You can change in the bath house there." The professor pointed to the white stucco structure at the back of the main house. He waited, playing nervously with his hands, until the sailor was gone, then squatted beside Beckman.

"You should see what he's got on underneath that uniform. Whoever designs those navy swim trunks really has the right idea. I mean, it's little better than a G string." Then quickly, apologetically, "Oh, I mean it's perfectly all right here. Almost nothing else will do, in fact. But out there, in public—"

"Maybe the kid can't afford anything else. You ought to keep that in mind."

"There's absolutely no need to be sarcastic, Beckman. What I really wanted to know was, where is Honey?"

Beckman shrugged. "I don't know."

The professor opened his mouth to say something further, but it faded away. Beckman saw it leave his face and mind, withdrawing like a ghost.

"You know, Leon, I've avoided it up until now, and I must admit you've been a perfect gentleman about it, but what really happened in New Orleans with Hoss?"

Leon compressed his lips. "Your friend Hoss is some kind of monster. I can tell you that, and that image he projects of the aggressive heterosexual is totally false." Leon waited, expecting his statement to have a strong effect on Beckman. "Well, he led me around by the nose for a few days, and then after he got what he wanted, he robbed me at knife point."

"Didn't you call the police?"

"Are you serious? You know what they do to people like me."

"Oh, I don't know, Leon. This is a very tolerant period in history. New Orleans has always had the reputation of being a rather open city."

"Not me. I'm not going to take a chance like that. I'll pay every time."

"Did Hoss say where he was going?" Beckman asked.

"To California, I suppose. He's insane enough. He ought to fit in there very well. If I had my way, dangerous people like that would be locked up."

The sailor was returning across the grass, walking slightly on his toes and wearing only his navy issue swim trunks. He pretended ignorance of the professor's scrutiny. Leon stood up quickly with undisguised rapture on his face.

"Better watch it, Leon. This boy may not be as naive as he appears."

Leon smiled down at Beckman. "I hope not."

The young sailor walked around to the diving board, tested it with a few springing hops, then did a near perfect jackknife dive, surfacing about midway down the pool, and swimming like a playful seal to the other end. The professor applauded. "Beautiful! Just beautiful!"

The young sailor was pleased with the admiration. As if expected to repeat the performance, he dove under again and started swimming with Tarzan-like breast strokes toward the other end of the pool.

"Don't you think you ought to at least warn him before you—"

"No!" Leon screamed. "No! You know I never force anybody. He will be free to leave any time he likes." Leon's face was enraged. "If you do anything to ruin this for me, I will kill you! I swear to God that I will kill you!"

The sailor surfaced at the other end, heaving for breath.

"Would you like a towel?" Leon shouted.

The sailor smiled and nodded yes.

"Just a second." Leon bent down once more next to Beckman. "Remember what I said. This is very important to me."

Beckman shrugged and watched as Leon picked up a towel

from one of the lounge chairs and walked hurriedly to where the sailor had climbed out of the pool. Beckman dove into the pool and swam leisurely over to the pool's ladder, climbed out, walked over to the outside shower, and washed the pool chemicals and the residual feeling of slime off his body. In the main house, he dressed in the new clothes Honey had bought for him; a pair of faded denim shorts, Roman sandals, and a large T-shirt with DO IT IN PALM BEACH printed in flashing colors on the front with appropriate sun and palm tree designs on the back. He poured a large rum over ice, squeezed half a lime into it, and flopped into one of Honey's cushioned bamboo chairs.

The house was an attractive place, a part of Honey's inheritance. Yet something about the place stubbornly rejected her. Her father's World War II mementos were still on display in the glass cases made for them, sealed in dustless air thirty years ago. A dented steel helmet, a long bayonet, a ragged, blood-stained Japanese Army shirt—all relics of a nearly forgotten brutality. When Beckman first opened the closet door in his room, he was shocked to see it half filled with old military uniforms, sagging from rusting hangers like a row of corpses.

In the corner of the closet stood a Belgian Army rifle. In another room, next to the kitchen, were rows and rows of preserved foods—all, Honey said, prepared by her mother in case of bombing.

Beckman had the disturbing feeling that he was sitting in the presence of very unfriendly ghosts. He imagined one of the guns suddenly falling out of its case and firing an ancient bullet at him. He finished his drink in a few gulps, stood up, looked around, almost believing that he would see an ethereal figure standing near him, ordering him out of their preserved time in a thunder-clap of rage. He felt his throat constricting—spiritual, weightless fingers closing off his breath, warning him. He left the house in a hurry;

not running, not walking, but moving swiftly down the palm-lined drive, past the iron gate and gasping only once, the way a scuba diver sucks in his first breath of surface air.

He walked down the street, ignoring the perpetual angry glances of Hispanic maids pushing baby strollers which held the white inheritors of vast fortunes. And he ignored the angry glances of those waiting for rides back to dirt and cheap food, back to horny Hispanic studs begging, "Hey, Mama, let's do it," and the unrelenting threat of poverty and of the powerful. In no other place that Beckman had seen were the differences between the rich and the poor so clearly drawn.

Beckman stopped to watch two young women strolling along in clean, tailored tennis outfits. They seemed like products of a separate species; naturally superior, haughty as angels, knowing secrets that only their equals could know.

A car squealed to a stop in front of him, slicing off his view of the two women. For an instant the car looked exactly like Malany's, smoking from the exhaust pipe, the body sagging on tired springs. Honey was behind the wheel, wearing a blonde Dutch Boy wig. There was something different about the car; not because it was a small difference, but because it was so big, like suddenly noticing that a whole group of stars were no longer visible. The top had been cut off, cut with a welder's acetylene torch, leaving burned, jagged edges and nodules of burnt, blue metal.

"You like that, huh!" Honey shouted, cutting her eyes toward the two women who were now only miniature figures in the distance. "You want to screw 'em?" Honey stood up in the seat and shouted in the direction of the women. "Hey, sweethearts, Beckman wants to fuck!"

Beckman leapt over the car door and jerked Honey down into the seat.

"What in the hell do you think you're doing? This car, that dumb wig, and doing what you did just now."

Honey shifted into low gear and started down the street toward the house.

"Was I convincing?"

"As what?"

"Zelda, of course. I've found the most wonderful suit for you. I had to go all over town before I found just the right thing. Navy blue with pinstripes and a stunning vest. I even stopped and bought you a carnation. See?"

She reached around in the back seat and brought out a flimsy, clear, plastic box containing a death white carnation.

"It'll look splendid on you, but you have to do something with your hair, lighten it a little, slick it back. You have to look super clean, you know, but also like you've got a splitting hangover and worried about impotency. That will be hardest for you, dear, but you must try."

"Honey, this is going too far. I'm not going to do it. It's a bit too much of a luxury, don't you think? Acting crazy without really being crazy."

"Well, how do you know I'm not 'really crazy,' as you say?"

"This is ridiculous. You're not insane, and you know it."

"Insane, no. But crazy, yes. There's a difference."

"I don't see it."

"Well, how can I explain it to you . . . let's see . . . The only way I can think of is that you've got to be a little crazy to keep from going insane. Understand?"

Honey turned into the driveway and rolled slowly into the garage. Beckman was silent, taken off balance by Honey's inverted reasoning. The sense was there, but then, when he thought about it, it wasn't.

"What about you and this psychokinesis stuff? That's crazy, ask anybody. How many people laugh in your face when you tell them?"

"Not many."

"That's bad. At least the ones who laugh aren't afraid of you. They don't think you're dangerous. You see, Beckman, we're a lot alike. We both have to do crazy things to keep from going insane. I sometimes think of it as aligning your perspectives. Now, come on. Get changed. I want to see what you look like as Scott Fitzgerald."

# CHAPTER 19

Beckman vowed to his image in the mirror that this would be the last time. No more of this perverse humiliation. He straightened his tie and brushed back his hair again. It would not lay down regardless of how much hair grease he put on it and, even though it made him slightly nauseous to think of it, he did look a little like Fitzgerald. One more tug at the vest and he walked out to the pool. Honey had torches burning around the pool and a seemingly endless tape of 1920s jazz music. Leon was there and Honey danced with the sailor.

He started to turn back. Private craziness with Honey he could tolerate, but group craziness had to be out of the question. A line had to be drawn.

Leon shouted from his table by the pool, "Wait. I want to talk to you."

Beckman stopped but did not turn around.

"Well, Scott, how do you like it?" Leon stepped back one pace, arms open for Beckman to admire his Alexander the Great costume.

"Very appropriate for conquest."

"Now, Beckman. Don't be churlish." The professor smiled. "Or is it jealous?"

"I have to go, Leon. Enjoy yourself."

"Wait, I didn't mean to be rude."

Leon cleared his throat. "It's really only a game, Beckman. Nothing serious, nothing to get angry about. Honey's even having a few guests over later. Everyone will be in costume. It'll be fun to watch. You know how Honey plays at reality the way others play at fantasy."

"You and the sailor weren't supposed to be here. Honey broke her promise," Beckman said, not bothering to disguise the irritation in his voice.

"Well, she's being Zelda, you know; zany, unpredictable, wild. I suppose she thinks that's a part of it."

"Maybe, but I've had enough of this madness. I'm leaving. Just do me one favor." Beckman said, pointing his finger at Leon's chest.

Leon smiled. "Of course."

"Give me an hour's head start before you tell her."

"You can count on it. In fact, I won't mention it to her at all if I can avoid it. I'm rather happy to see you go."

"I know."

Beckman turned and walked away, straight to Honey's room. She had left her purse on the bed, along with her undergarments and a wadded-up dress. He tore open the purse, jabbed his hand down into it, and scattered the contents until he felt the wallet. He jerked it out, took out all of the cash, grabbed two sets of keys off the dresser, and ran for the garage.

He drove as fast as the speed limit would allow to the airport in West Palm Beach, parked the car in the first available place, left the keys in it, and walked hurriedly to the terminal building. Airports had always been exotic places to him, so he didn't feel too conspicuous in the Fitzgerald suit, running from airline counter to airline counter, searching for the earliest departure for Memphis. He found one leaving in thirty minutes.

He assumed Leon had already told her. There would be enough time for Honey to come after him and cause a scene worthy of the most fanatical skyjacker. He would have to take the chance. He bought a one-way ticket, practically ran through the metal detecting arch, and ignored the suspicious looks of the attendant when he told her that he didn't have a bag.

At the gate, he leaned against a stanchion where he could see out into the terminal building. People were still walking through the security arch like some gateway to eternity. The thought frightened him; the possibility of crashing—few people survive when those massive iron birds plummet to the earth.

He had never flown before, and the thought of it now began to nauseate him. There was still time to catch a bus, still time to walk back through that archway. Maybe he could cash in his ticket, but then the announcement to board came; commanding, reassuring. The group that he was to fly with, and possibly to die with, rose en masse and, bunching together, waited their turn to walk through the narrow hallway to the plane. Each was greeted by a blonde flight attendant who scanned them from head to toe with front to back scrutiny, then flicked an approving smile as they entered the tubular body of the aircraft.

Beckman took his place beside the window. He could look out at the slender, knife-like wing supporting incongruously bulky engines. He felt oddly privileged to have this seat. The other two passengers beside him had to deal with a strictly human environment. He could escape out of the window, as close to real cosmic space as he was ever going to be.

The door was sealed. Beckman gasped. There was no physical escape now. The man next to him, who could have represented any suit and tie occupation, immediately opened a paperback book. He was used to it. The unimaginable mystery of the machine no longer interested him. The airplane's hard, silver brightness, its violent potential were as disturbing to him as the picture of the half-naked woman on the cover of his book who seemed to look on some unshown horror.

The plane started to roll. Beckman watched the wing outside of his window change shape. Hard, straight-lined, mechanical parts, without the delicate touch of feathers, extended and retracted with non-fluid economy. Who were these mathematicians and engineers that could create such powerful states of dynamic equilibrium? Was it because they had an unshakable belief in the absolute correctness of their logic? Were the symbols they worked with more than just abstract representations? Beckman looked out again at the wing which had now become more like a slender, metallic finger, an unnatural thing, touching the setting sun.

Beckman could see no human life on the earth below. There was hardly an indication that it even existed, except for an occasional cluster of small buildings, looking more like rubble. He was in a world of sky and cloud, inhabited only by him and the people with him. He was sorry now that he had insisted on driving to Palm Beach when Honey wanted to fly.

He had wanted to waste time on the way, hoping that an opportunity would come, an acceptable opportunity like some natural disaster—a flood in Memphis or a crazed killer stalking Palm Beach—would call the trip off.

He and Honey had made three motel stops along the way to Palm Beach. Beckman combed the national papers at every stop but found nothing, not even a reported fire. At the last stop, Beckman crawled out of bed when he was convinced Honey was asleep, and called Leon back in Memphis, who in a voice seething with rage—it was three a.m.—told Beckman in chopped-off words that no one had called, mailed, or begged for him, Malany or anything else, and hung up. Leon flew down later, for a long weekend, and was very apologetic.

Beckman's existence down on earth seemed very remote from his seat in the plane. It seemed really pointless and trivial, more like the life of a primitive organism running away from or going to some stimulus. He wanted, for a moment, to stay in the plane. He envied the flight crew, their life spent floating between earth and space, to the point of tears. Thinking about the landing depressed him, so he ordered two drinks and, hoping to impress the stony gentleman next to him, drank from both three-ounce bottles simultaneously.

It was fully dark when the airplane touched down on earth again. Beckman hurried through the deplaning routine and through the terminal. He hailed the first cab he saw and gave the driver Honey's address. The driver maintained the speed limits and drove very efficiently, the only cab driver he had ever ridden with who didn't treat an automobile and traffic rules like natural enemies, and it had to happen when Beckman was in the most desperate hurry of his life.

Beckman seemed moved into a kind of Doppler world from the speed and instantaneousness of the jet to the slowing down of a receding howl. The cab seemed to barely roll along, stopping at innumerable traffic lights, gaggles of pedestrians, yield signs, stop signs, and speed signs. Beckman had never before fully realized the complexity of simply driving a car. For a moment, he briefly considered jumping out and running; at least the illusion of speed, of action, would be preferable to the agony of sitting innocuously in the back seat of a law-abiding cab.

He tossed a $5 bill over the front seat even before the cab came to a stop in front of Honey's house. The place was dark except for the yellow illumination of the streetlight. Beckman hurried up the driveway to the side door. He tried the keys but they did not fit. He then tried the front door, then the back, but nothing worked.

It was just like her to remove them, Beckman thought. He even considered the possibility that this had been a part of some elaborate plan of Honey's, a clever and intelligent way of demonstrating her power.

He went back to the side door and, with the useless keys, broke out the windowpane next to the lock. He reached through the shattered glass and around to the lock and turned the bolt. A dog barked from somewhere nearby, in the darkness. The explosiveness of the sounds caused him to jump and cut his hand on the glass. The animal's awareness of his presence accelerated his sense of urgency close to panic. He pushed open the door and ran, stumbling, through the darkened house.

He knocked over objects and fumbled for light switches until he found the stairs leading up to the bedrooms. He charged up the stairs, burst into Honey's bedroom and began wildly collecting his clothes, stuffing them into his duffle bag and, for some reason still unknown to him, then began switching off all of the lights. Once again, he stumbled in the dark to the side door, closed it behind him, and relocked it.

He leapt down from the small side porch. The duffle bag snagged on something, and the energy of his weight pulled it over on top of him, striking his head first, then slamming across his back. Beckman wrestled the bag onto the ground, wildly kicking and pushing until the bag lay quiet and dead beside him. Then, as though he had been rehearsing the scene known to everyone but himself, he scrambled to his feet, stunned and confused. He irrationally brushed the dirt from his suit. With the bag under control, he began to run, dragging and bumping it along. Something caused him to stop; a voice, a sound? He waited in the tense silence. Then an explosion of lights enveloped him, blinded him, and nearly beat him back down to the ground. He covered his eyes with both arms. A voice from beyond the ring of terrible white rays demanded that he halt and put his hands up.

Beckman could not take his arms away from his face. The hideous light penetrated everywhere. It blazed through the threads of his suit and it even appeared to glow like a red X-ray through the flesh of his arm, outlining delicate bones and a nexus of veins, nerves, and arteries.

Powerful hands jerked his arms away and held them straight out on each side. He squeezed his eyes shut against the light until he could see only two opaque red ovals. The pain which had shot through to the back of his head lessened. Something, or someone, jerked him up to a standing position with his arms still pulled out into tight bands. A pair of hands indelicately fondled his body. A hard voice, reeking of old cigarettes, shouted next to his ear to someone behind the lights, "He's clean." The high intensity lights switched off and smaller, more subtle flashlights probed his face. Steel-jawed manacles locked around his wrists.

"Buddy, you're under arrest for breaking and entering. Read him the shit," the same voice said; the same voice that had been behind the lights.

The man with cigarette breath held a worn card up to his flashlight and read, in a hurried monotone, an unintelligible list of Beckman's rights as a suspected felon. The man's breath sickened him, and the blow on his head from the duffle bag made his brain slosh inside of its cranial tomb. He couldn't have stopped the compelling release of the contents of his stomach even if he had tried.

The policeman reading from the "rights" card, failed to see the warning signs and Beckman spewed forth a column of foul, hot, chunky liquid. The policeman jumped back but continued reading from the card, speeding his voice up to Donald Duck rapidity, then saying, "Son of a bitch. Somebody give me a towel. He got it all over my shoes."

Laughter was all around Beckman.

"Well, who's he going to go with?" another voice asked.

"Not me," Cigarette Breath quickly injected. "If he shits in his pants, I want it to get on somebody else."

More laughter.

"Come on, boy," a different voice said, and someone grabbed him by the arm, pulled him to a dark police car, opened the rear door, and shoved him in.

The ride to the police station was mostly in silence, except for the last few miles when the policemen started to complain about the smell of the vomit.

"Take him upstairs and get him cleaned up," the older man in the right seat told the driver.

Beckman was led through the wide door at the rear of the station where they had parked in a large police parking lot. The driver, a pale-faced man of about forty, held on lightly to Beckman's arm and pointed him up one flight of stairs to the men's toilet. Inside the toilet, the policeman unlocked the manacles and waited—lips compressed, one hand resting on his nightstick, the other on his bullet belt—while Beckman washed his face and hands and diligently wiped at the spots on his tie and jacket with a paper towel.

The policeman's cap bill covered his eyes, and his uniform seemed segmented by crossing vertical and horizontal lines. Beckman felt a painful contraction of his genitals. He was in the grip of some terrible force, mindless and deadly as a raging tyrannosaur. The reflection of the policeman in the mirror, the white florescent light, the white walls and white toilet fixtures seemed, and he truly believed, inescapable. He had a couple of dry heaves before turning to the policeman who re-handcuffed him and, staying within arm's reach, motioned him toward the door.

They walked down the lower hall, also shimmering in white light, and entered an elevator. The elevator stopped at the first floor where a muscular black man in a torn shirt and hands cuffed behind him was escorted by two policemen. They stepped into the elevator. The door closed and the elevator started up when the black man started screaming, full volume, and charged, head-first, against the elevator door. Beckman and his escort flattened themselves against the back side of the elevator while the black man's escorts tried to subdue him.

The black man was very strong, naturally strong, and the madness he directed at breaking down the elevator door was now turned against his antagonists. He started kicking. One kick caught a policeman on the side of his leg. He groaned but did not drop. The black man seemed to be all moving legs and bobbing head.

There was a short hiss like the stroke of a tire pump, and Beckman's eyes felt filled with sand and fire. His throat constricted and he, along with all the occupants of the elevator, erupted into spasms of wild coughing. Then the door opened, sounding like an explosion, and everyone burst out into a top floor lobby.

"Why in the goddamn hell did you use that, and in an elevator?" one of the policemen demanded.

"Now there's no use to get that way about it. What the hell did you expect me to do with this crazy asshole? He'd already taken you out. If I'd waited for him to use that foot on me, he'd have raised my voice to a squeak for the rest of my life. If I'd had my old blackjack, I wouldn't have had to use this shit."

He slapped contemptuously at his mace holster. He turned to Beckman's escort. "Sometimes you just can't get along without an old-fashioned blackjack. Know what I mean?"

Beckman's escort nodded but remained erect, even while wiping the chemical tears from his cheeks. The black man's escorts traded accusations for a moment, then led the man away.

Watching the black man go to his fate, Beckman knew with immutable awareness that here everything was real, that the craziness outside, whether wonderful or terrible, would be—if it were captured—bludgeoned, gassed, stomped, or electrocuted out of existence. Absolute sanity ruled Beckman's actions, and he was more afraid now than at any time since he and Malany fled from Herschel and the restaurant.

As they walked down another white, luminous hall, past innumerable closed doors without so much as a scratch to distinguish them, Beckman felt, and truly believed, that Honey, with her veiled superiority, had planned this for him all along. He had been helpless and without hope from the very beginning, like all experimental animals, and this is where it would end.

# CHAPTER 20

After Beckman had handed in his breakfast tray, he strode back to the corner of the cell where he had spent the night. His thinking was a little clearer now, less fractured by his own mental spasms of self-reproach and the exterior shouts from other cells. There had been a fight in the next cell during the night. He could hear the grunts and blows of the combatants. No one came in to stop it. The last policeman he saw was the one who had walked him to the cell. No one even cheered the fight on. The grunts and blows simply went on until they stopped, and were replaced by the night noises of squeaking beds and regular breathing.

Beckman squatted in the corner, thinking. His cellmate, staring at him from darkened caves, kept his worn and spotted coat pulled close to his body, even though it was hot in the cell.

Beckman stared back and, with a surge of daring, asked the man, "What are you here for?"

The man, without changing his expression—he had no expression to begin with—said through ventriloquist lips, "Food and shelter."

"You mean you got arrested so that you could come here to eat and sleep?"

The man nodded. "It used to be easy. All you had to do was stagger down the street and they would pick you up, but now—I had to get on the bus and go all the way to Germantown. I staggered around out there about fifteen minutes before they came and got me. It's getting to be a real problem. I don't do it much, you know, not like some of the other fellas who are always trying to get in here. I just do it whenever I really need a square meal and can't find it no other way."

"One thing I've always wanted to ask men like you."

"Men like me?" the cellmate repeated, with a smile.

"How did it happen? How did you end up like this?"

"You've asked the wrong man, my friend. You should ask them." The man swept his arm toward the cell door and window, "They'd know better than I would. All I seem to remember is one day realizing that I didn't care about anything. They could do what they wanted to me." He swept his arms toward the window again. "And I didn't give a real damn. I figured I'd be dead in a week, but that didn't happen. I've lived like this for ten years now, and still don't give a damn." The man stared at Beckman more intensely and, with a smile, said, "Young man, I think we have a lot in common."

Beckman was struck with horror. He crouched back in his corner, his former courage gone. The cellmate stared at him for a long time, then climbed into his bunk and lay facing the wall.

Beckman trembled in the heat of his corner. The prophetic truth of the man's words resounded in his head, obliterating thought as well as standing beliefs, invalidated memory, and pounded with demonic force at the walls of his heart.

For a moment the sound of the jailer calling his name was terribly confusing. He hesitated to answer but when the jailer showed himself in front of his cell, red-faced and angry, and shouted his name with finality, Beckman jumped up and lurched out of his cell.

He followed the jailer down through the cell area, possibly to his death, or to a beating, to torture, to God knows what, but he was happy, almost to tears, to be out of the cell and free from his cellmate. He decided, in that brief walk to the jailer's office, that he would gladly accept death, even insist on it, rather than go back to that cell.

Honey was waiting in the jailer's office, dressed in the Park

Avenue fashions of the '20s. Seeing her so confident, so able, he gasped with pure joy. He rushed over to her, jerked her gloved hand to his lips and began kissing it.

"Please, Beckman," she slowly withdrew her hand. "The gentleman has something for you to sign."

The jailer dropped into a swivel seat behind his desk, "You have been released to this lady's custody for a period of—"

"Yes, yes. What do I sign? This?" Beckman pulled one of the papers on the desk toward him.

"Now hold on, wait a minute, boy; goddamn if you ain't anxious." The jailer laughed and, looking at Honey, shoved a folder of papers toward Beckman.

"You see how it is, ma'am. I tell you, if everybody had to spend at least one night in jail, there wouldn't be no more trouble in this world."

Beckman signed everything before him, giggling like a rescued castaway, and accepted joyfully, without checking the contents, the small envelope containing his personal effects.

"Don't be so polite, sweetheart, you're saved. I saved you," Honey cooed.

Beckman wiped tears from his cheeks and thanked her again.

"But, you see, there are conditions."

Beckman nodded and let his head dangle after the last nod.

"You see, dear, I paid your bail and had you released into my custody, guaranteeing your appearance in court on the proper date. Oh, of course you will not have to go to court; that is, unless you do something as hurtful as you did at Palm Beach and force me not to drop the charges. Running off like that during the party. It was very embarrassing, and I must say I was a little angry at the affront. I knew you would return to pick up that smelly old army bag, so I checked the flight that I thought you would probably take. You know, the earliest one. Then I calculated how long the cab ride would take and then called the police. I was really in a sweat, dear, for a while, wondering if the timing was right. But, you see, everything worked out perfectly."

Beckman resumed nodding. They walked across the police parking lot to her car. Beckman was slightly behind her. She had on a wide brimmed hat of pre-World War I style.

"Oh, and there's one other thing, dear. You signed your own bail bond agreement which means that if you do something foolish again, the bondsman will come and get you. And, from the look of the character I dealt with, I wouldn't advise leaving until he's paid."

Beckman nodded and followed her quietly to the car.

"It's early morning yet, dear. Let's go for a drive until lunch. I know just the place."

They climbed into the wax-smelling Model A, and Beckman felt the comfortable pleasure of its leather-covered seats and the solid, definite, metal locking sounds of the doors. Honey started the engine, listened to its gentle tapping rhythm for a minute, then started off. Beckman settled comfortably in the seat, almost overjoyed. He grinned and inhaled deeply, the warm Memphis air beating past his face.

"I'm so glad you still have your suit on. I was really afraid they would put you in dungarees or one of those awful jumpsuits. Straighten up your tie, dear, and you would be a perfect Henry James."

Beckman straightened his tie.

"And who do you think I am?" Honey asked.

Beckman wrinkled his brow theatrically and said. "Edith Wharton?"

"Oh, that's right. Wonderful, you're catching on."

"What about sex, Honey? You'll have to give it up." Beckman thought he saw a counter.

"Only with my husband and, as you know, that was never a problem . . . Oh, by the way, read this."

She thrust a wrinkled letter at him. Beckman read. It was a short letter and, despite the bouncing and lurching of the Model A, he was able to read it quickly:

Dearest Honey,

This will come as a surprise to you, as it certainly did to me. And, believe me, I thought a long time before making this decision. Actually, it wasn't a question of whether I was going to do it, since the first time I laid eyes on Todd, I knew what I wanted, and that I was going to get it. The problem was, how was I going to tell you?

I know that what I'm going to do will destroy our little setup, but let's face it, dear, it couldn't last forever. Things were bound to happen.

And happen they did: When I met Todd, I knew that it was the purest love. I am ecstatic, delirious with happiness. For the first time in my life—and it's nearly half over, you know—I found something real and lasting. I feel like a real person. I know how corny that sounds, but it's true. Now that I think back at how I was, I don't even recognize myself. No more icy, dead cynicism, no more anger. It's wonderful. I only hope that, someday, you can experience what I have. Then maybe you'll understand. I hope so, dear, for your sake. Please try not to be too angry.

Yours Sincerely,
Leon

P.S. All I know is that I want to spend the rest of my life with Todd, and he feels the same.

Beckman handed the letter back to Honey who laughed, hooting like a boat horn.

"You know, at first I could have killed him, but then I saw he was right. The show couldn't last. He did the right thing. And now I've got you." She smiled. "A much more agreeable arrangement."

Yes, it was an agreeable arrangement even as he thought about it, an inevitable arrangement. All those giant, unrelenting forces that had hounded him from every shadow, forces that he realized now were always unescapable, had at last focused on him in this time and place. Beckman felt a profound sense of gratitude that he had, for some inexplicable reason, been spared the final knowledge. It had come very close, and he had been in its dark, terrible presence. But "Thank God," he muttered, he had not seen it.

"What?" Honey said. "What did you say?"

"Oh, it was nothing, Honey. Really. Nothing."

"Good," Honey said with finality. "Now don't worry. You can start writing again or you can even open up that parapsychology clinic you've talked about."

"I mentioned that?"

"Yes, you did . . . I'm sure you did."

"Ha, I don't remember it."

"Well, it doesn't matter, darling. The future is yours. You can do anything you want." She smiled. "With certain restrictions, of course."

"Of course," Beckman answered, returning the smile.

Honey turned down Riverside Drive and headed for the bridge. Beckman hunched down in the seat, resting his knees against the antique dash. He understood better what happens in the mind of a hooded falcon.

"Let's run over to West Memphis, dear. There are a few antique shops there where I've always been lucky. Would you mind?"

Beckman shrugged and, for the first time in his life, thought it would be a good idea to start smoking. He decided, in fact, that at the first stop he would buy his first pack of cigarettes, possibly even make a ceremony out of it.

Honey had merged into the bridge traffic, westbound, still ticking along in the slow traffic lane. The air, still hot and dense, smelled of water and crushed green leaves.

"I've always detested Arkansas. You know, as an idea but . . ."

"Wait! Wait!" Beckman shouted. "Look!" He pointed to the stalled traffic on the eastbound side of the bridge.

Traffic had stopped in all lanes, some rested at angles where they had apparently skidded across the lanes. Most people were standing out of their cars or standing on bumpers, on tops of hoods and trunks; all watching the gaunt solitary figure dressed in black at the bridge railing. The figure looked toward the sky.

"Stop!" Beckman shouted.

Honey tapped the brakes in more of a reflex action, then jerked her foot away. "Not on the bridge, Beckman. It's dangerous and besides, I think it's illegal."

"Well, do something: Go across the river then, and turn around on the other side," Beckman shouted.

Honey moved over to the left lane, heedless of other cars frantically braking or making wild, evasive turns. Honey turned at the first cut-through and drove up to the end of the traffic line.

"My God, Beckman. I didn't know you had such a morbid fascination with things like this."

Beckman jumped out of the car and ran through the waiting lanes of cars, most with engines running to keep their air conditioners going, and pushed aside the thickening crowd with surprising audacity, ignoring the shouts and curses from behind, until his chest collided with the outstretched arm of a policeman.

"Sir, I know that person. I'm a friend of hers," Beckman half-screamed at the policeman.

The policeman scrutinized him with mixed disbelief. Beckman had decided instantly to break past the policeman and take his chances, but the policeman took him by the arm and led him toward a group of other policemen, gathered next to an official-looking car. All looked toward the figure at the bridge rail. Beckman's policeman said something serious to him, but he could not hear because of the crowd shouting.

"They're mad because they think you're some kind of privileged character. Afraid somebody's getting ahead of 'em. Ain't that something?"

The policeman looked back at the crowd. "Get back, goddammit, or I'll run you all in!" he shouted. "Sir, this man says he knows the jumper."

The man in charge pushed back his gold-encrusted hat, smiled, and said, "Well, get him out there. We got to do something before this crowd gets any bigger. And listen," the high-ranking policeman spoke like a demanding father to Beckman's policeman. "Let the boys know to keep any of those goddamn bloodthirsty news people away, you hear? Once this thing gets on the news, every goddamn preacher and everybody in both states who can walk or crawl will be here."

Beckman's policeman released his grip. Beckman, not waiting for further discussion, ran as hard as he could to Malany. He was nearly out of breath when he reached her, and for a long while stood beside her, breathing hard, trying to speak.

"Beckman," she said, "I was hoping I would see you again."

"You could have answered more of my calls. God, Malany, my cries."

"You wouldn't have recognized me, Beckman. I'm a different person now." She hesitated, glanced at the river. "Not better, not anything really. Just different."

"I wouldn't have cared, Malany. We could have still gone to California together. We could have made something of ourselves there."

Malany shook her head. "No. I know who I am now. There's no need, and it would be useless to try."

"They sent me up here to stop you, Malany."

She laughed. "Isn't that funny? I have no intention of doing anything. I never had. We were only driving over the bridge, coming back from a therapeutic outing, talking about what happened. Then I saw this view of the river, the wonderful Mississippi, and the city in the background, and it was the most beautiful thing . . . " Her voice cracked, her eyes moistened. "I had to. I felt like I had to keep looking at it. So we stopped, just to look. That's all. And then, the next thing I realized, there was the crowd behind me. People were shouting things. Then the police came, and that's the way it's been. You're the only one who's dared to come this close."

"They all think you're going to jump, Malany."

"Yes, I know. To tell you the truth, the thought never really crossed my mind. But now, looking back at them, it doesn't seem like a bad idea, does it?"

Beckman leaned over the rail and looked down at the turbulent, muddy water. "It would hurt when you hit. I wouldn't like that, plus not to mention the suffocation and then, that final step."

"That's true, and you know, yesterday I would have jumped and not given a second thought about it. But today, in just twenty-four hours, I've finally realized who I am. He knew all along."

She nodded back toward the prominent black Lincoln Continental stopped in the first row of cars.

"It's kinda sad, you know, but he has always known me better than I knew myself." She looked down at the swirling water and was silent for a few moments. "But that's over now."

"You mean you're not going back to him?"

"Oh, no. I'm going back to him. I have to."

"Malany, what happened with John Darling?"

She laughed quietly and looked at the sky. "Let's see. I can't remember what we talked about because what we said meant nothing. We talked about nothing. He was a great cook and loved meat dishes particularly. So, I ate meat. We ate and ate and then smoked and snorted and drank until we were delirious, but never irretrievably. That's what made it so difficult. He pretended to read my stuff and shout about its greatness, said he would get me a good publisher, and then we would screw and screw and screw. All of a sudden, I was what I was before, and I had the terrible feeling that my little poetess trip was only a joke." Again, she nodded toward the Lincoln. "I realize now that Darling spotted it, but lied so that he could get me into bed. Honey laughed at it, Hoss sensed it. Only you, Beckman, believed, like some little naive child. I'll always treasure you for it. I won't forget you." She hesitated and then said, "Tell me, Beckman, have you ever been in love?"

Beckman looked out at the churning brown water of the Mississippi. "No," he said. "I don't think so." He then reached over and took her hand. "Please, Malany. Let's leave now. Let's continue on. Let's hit California like a storm."

She smiled. "No, Beckman. It isn't possible. I've come as far as I can go." She withdrew her hand slowly.

"Just tell me why, Malany, why are you going back to him—to that life of self-centered materialism he's offering you."

Malany smiled slightly and shrugged. "What else does a wounded animal do, but crawl back to where it felt safe? Take care of yourself, kid, and stick with Honey as long as you can. You're safe with her, at least for a while."

Beckman watched as she walked back toward the crowd and the long, black Continental, and watched as the large, dark-clad man sitting in the rear opened the door.

Beckman turned and looked once again at the river. Something big was floating in the water, something long and black, made shiny from the water washing over it. It moved steadily with the current, unaffected by the brown eddies around the bridge. As it moved farther away, Beckman saw that it was a large truck tire, but he couldn't truly be sure.

This was the river of Huck Finn and Tom Sawyer, the very aorta of America, and he looked at the city where so much happened every day and every night without causing a significant ripple in the water.

He walked back to the relieved group of police officers who slapped him on the back and said that he did a good job and that he would be recommended by them for a citizen's award. Beckman thanked them and walked back to Honey's car.

They rode back to Honey's house with Beckman listening sporadically to Honey's tattletale chatter, in the manner of Edith Wharton, and her phony praise of his courage and self-sacrifice. She promised rewards, she said, that he couldn't begin to imagine. But all Beckman could think of was the word, *Quiet*.

## ABOUT THE AUTHOR

A retired Aviation Safety Inspector for the FAA, Daniel V. Meier, Jr. has always had a passion for writing. During his college years, he studied history at the University of North Carolina, Wilmington (UNCW), American Literature at the University of Maryland Graduate School, an in 1980 was published by Leisure Books under the pen name of Vince Daniels.

He also worked for the Washington Business Journal as a journalist and has been a contributing writer/editor for several aviation magazines. His historical action/adventure, *The Dung Beetles of Liberia* was released in September 2019.

Dan and his wife live in Owings, Maryland, about twenty miles south of Annapolis and when he's not writing, they spend their summers sailing on the Chesapeake Bay.

## OTHER BOOKS BY DANIEL V. MEIER, JR.

Based on the remarkable true account of a young American who landed in Liberia in 1961.

NOTHING COULD HAVE PREPARED HIM FOR THE EVENTS HE WAS ABOUT TO EXPERIENCE. Ken Verrier quickly realizes the moment he arrives in Liberia that he is in a place where he understand very little of what is considered normal, where the dignity of life has little meaning, and where he can trust no one.

It's 1961 and young Ken Verrier is experiencing the turbulence of Ishmael and the guilt of his brother's death. His sudden decision to drop out of college and deal with his demons shocks his family, his friends, and especially his girlfriend, soon to have been his fiancee. His destination: Liberia—the richest country in Africa both in monetary wealth and natural resources.

Author Daniel Meier describes Ken Verrier's many escapades, spanning from horrifying to whimsical, with engaging and fast-moving narrative that ultimately describe a society upon which the wealthy are feeding and in which the poor are being buried.

It's a novel that will stay with you long after the last word has been read.

## RELEASING IN AUGUST 2021

**A gripping account of survival in America's earliest settlement, Jamestown, Virginia.**

Virginia, 1622. Powhatan warriors prepare war paint from the sacred juice of the bloodroot plant, but Nehiegh, the English son-in-law of Chief Ochawintan has sworn never to kill again. He must leave before the massacre.

England 1609. Matthew did not trust his friend, Richard's stories of Paradise in the Jamestown settlement, but nothing could have equipped him for the violence and privation that awaited him in this savage land.

Once ashore in the fledging settlement, Matthew experiences the unimaginable beauty of this pristine land and learns the meaning of hope, but it all turns into a nightmare as gold mania infests the community and Indians become an increasing threat. The nightmare only gets worse as the harsh winter brings on "the starting time" and all the grizzly horrors of a desperate and dying community that come with it.

Driven to the depths of despair by the guilt of his sins against Richard and his lust for that man's wife, Matthew seeks death.

In that moment of crisis, when he chooses death over a life of depravity, he unexpectedly finds new life among his sworn enemy, the Powhatan Indians.

What will this new life mean for Matthew, and will he survive?